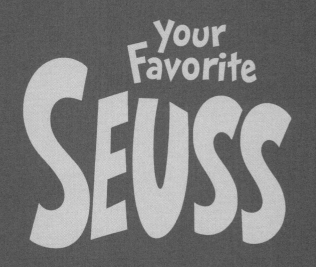

Your Favorite Seuss

13 stories written and illustrated by Dr. Seuss
with 13 introductory essays

*compiled by Janet Schulman
and Cathy Goldsmith*

DESIGNED BY MOLLY LEACH

RANDOM HOUSE 🏠 NEW YORK

Many thanks to Audrey Geisel; Herb Cheyette, agent for Dr. Seuss; and Lynda Corey Claassen, Director of the Mandeville Special Collections Library, University of California, San Diego, for making this book possible.

Special thanks to the authors of the essays preceding each story and to the members of Our Lady of Lourdes High School Environmental Club for the help they gave Pete Seeger: Mike McCann, Danielle Monaco, Kelly O'Connell, Maria Oldiges, Peter Paggi, Kaileen Rohr, Stasha Rosen, Steve Russomano, Laura Sabia, Rebecca Trama, John Varallo, and faculty advisor Joseph Timms.

Library of Congress Cataloging-in-Publication Data
Seuss, Dr.
Your favorite Seuss / [compiled] by Janet Schulman and Cathy Goldsmith ; illustrated by Dr. Seuss and with photographs by miscellaneous photographers.
   p. cm.
SUMMARY: A compilation of more than a dozen previously published Dr. Seuss books, plus thirteen essays by authors and other book lovers, including Audrey Geisel, widow of Dr. Seuss.
ISBN 0-375-81061-7
1. Humorous stories, American. 2. Children's stories, American. [1. Humorous stories. 2. Stories in rhyme.
3. Short stories.] I. Schulman, Janet. II. Goldsmith, Cathy. III. Seuss, Dr., Selections. IV. Title.
PZ8.3.G5738You 2004 [E]—dc22 2004001288

CONTENTS

who is dr. seuss? Introduction by Janet Schulman

stories and essays

who is dr. seuss?

Born on March 2, 1904, in Springfield, Massachusetts, he was christened Theodor Seuss Geisel, Seuss being the maiden name of his mother. Some twenty years later the witty collegian began signing some of his drawings in the Dartmouth humor magazine with the name Seuss. A few years after that, as a successful cartoonist in leading humor magazines of the time, he added Dr. to Seuss, a tongue-in-cheek reference to the doctorate in literature he blew off when he dropped out of Oxford University to doodle full-time. Today Theodor Geisel is known to all Americans and a goodly portion of the rest of the world as Dr. Seuss. But to Cathy Goldsmith and me—and to everyone who personally knew him—he was simply Ted.

Cathy and I had the privilege of working with Ted at Random House during the last eleven years of his life, Cathy as his art director and I as his editor. We often are asked, "What was he like?" He was in his mid-seventies by the time we started working together and, since he lived in La Jolla, California, and we were in New York City, we didn't get to see him as often as we would have liked. But when he did come to New York, his sly sense of humor always came with him, and toward the end of his life, when we went to La Jolla, he still was able to make us laugh. Tall and elegant, ramrod-straight with a handsome

head of slicked-back silver hair, he could have passed for an aristocratic European ambassador. Who would have thought this distinguished gentleman was a down-to-earth funnyman without an ounce of pretense in his body, our own homegrown American ambassador of humor? Maybe the twinkle in his eye would have given him away.

But I am not sure that Cathy and I or many others really knew Ted Geisel. He was a very private person who did not talk about himself. A bit of a recluse, he was thought by some to be shy, but I think it is more likely that he was bored with most people's small talk and avoided social situations where he would have to

listen to it. One thing he did have was stage fright. That can be traced to the unjustified humiliation he suffered at age fourteen when former president Theodore Roosevelt came to Springfield to pin medals on ten Boy Scouts, but when he got to Ted, the last boy on stage, he had no more medals. Roosevelt bellowed out, "What is this little boy doing here?" That little boy never quite got over it.

Much as Ted hated being in the spotlight, there were times when he simply had to, most notably to accept his ever-increasing awards and honorary degrees. But he made sure that he wouldn't have to be at the podium for more than a minute or two. His speeches were in verse and short, yet they were always memorable.

In spite of his ban on appearing on television, Ted did suffer through a good number of press interviews. One of the questions he frequently got was, "Where do you get your ideas?" At some point he concocted an answer and delivered it with deadpan sincerity: he got his ideas in Über Gletch, a small hamlet in the Swiss Alps, where he went each summer to get his cuckoo clock fixed. It annoyed Ted that many of these same journalists would describe his books as "whimsical." Ted once said to me, "'Whimsical' means that the books say nothing. Look it up in the dictionary. It means capricious, without reason." There was not a book that Ted wrote that did not have something to say. And as for where he got his ideas, he got them the same place most good authors get theirs: from within himself, and most probably from trolling the deepest wellsprings of his childhood in Springfield.

His books fall into two categories, the ones we call his "big" books being several inches wider and taller than Beginner Books, his other type of book. The "big" books gave us Marco from Mulberry Street and Bartholomew of the many hats; Horton the faithful elephant, who went on to save the tiny world of Who-ville; the snooty Sneetches and Yertle the bully turtle; the Yooks and the Zooks, who were ready to go to war over the correct way to eat buttered bread; the Grinch, who tried to stop Christmas; the Lorax, who spoke for the trees; Thidwick the big-hearted moose; and so many other purely invented characters. Most of them have "messages" of moral or ethical import embedded in the funny stories. Dr. Seuss was the best kind of teacher—virtually invisible. And that, I think, was because he did not consciously write for children but rather for himself. No condescension, no talking down, no preaching. Some of his books are simply journeys of self-discovery, of using your imagination to take you to places where no mind has gone before.

Beginner Books, launched with *The Cat in the Hat* in 1957, are dedicated to making learning to read fun. They differ from the "big" books not only in size. The vocabulary is restricted to words children would be expected to learn to read during their first year of school, and just about every sentence is illustrated, thus providing visual clues to the meaning of words.

TED HOLDING A LION CUB AT SPRINGFIELD ZOO, 1938.

And yet even with these strict guidelines, the good doctor was able to pull out of his bag one wonderfully funny, action-packed story after another.

It is impossible to say what is more important in a Dr. Seuss book, the words or the illustrations, because they are inseparable. He gave us new words—"nerd" and "Grinch," to name but two—and when no word existed to complete a rhyme, he would make one up. I think he must have had a lot of fun playing with words in *If I Ran the Zoo*. One of my favorite verses in that menagerie of Gerald McGrew's imagination is:

And, speaking of birds,
there's the Russian Palooski,
Whose headski is redski and belly is blueski.
I'll get one of them for my Zooski McGrewski.

I marvel at how effortless Ted made his writing seem. The words trip off one's tongue. Few people know how hard he worked—rewriting and rewriting and rewriting—to get the words just right.

And not to be outdone in the word department, Dr. Seuss's loopy illustrations are as much fun as the stories. Though three of his books—*McElligot's Pool, Bartholomew and the Oobleck,* and *If I Ran the Zoo*—were named Caldecott Honor Books by the American Library Association, none won the coveted gold Caldecott Medal. Perhaps his illustrations were *too* original for Caldecott Committees' taste. But he was always a great favorite of children's librarians, and in 1980 ALA honored him with the Laura Ingalls Wilder Medal for his "lasting contribution to literature for children."

Selecting the books to be included in *Your Favorite Seuss* was not easy. Cathy and I wished this book could have been twice as long—but we also wanted a book that a child could lift! I have to confess that neither Cathy nor I have one favorite. Two of Cathy's have been included—*Happy Birthday to You!* and *McElligot's Pool*. Three of mine have been included—*McElligot's Pool, The Sneetches,* and *The Cat in the*

Hat. I don't think that most Dr. Seuss fans do have one single book that stands out above all others as their absolute favorite. So it is our hope that we have included many favorites, knowing all too well that some fans' beloved books are missing.

Though we have included all of the words and virtually all of the illustrations, we do not intend this treasury to be a replacement for the experience of reading and looking at the original books. If, as your family uses this treasury, you discover a certain story that must be read night after night after night, I urge you to purchase the original. It may be the book your child will take to college and keep forever. It is also our hope that families who know Dr. Seuss only through his very popular Beginner Books will discover in this collection some of his less familiar but meatier "big" books. Or perhaps be inspired to check out others that are not in this volume.

Each of the stories is prefaced with a brief essay by a person whose life has been touched by Dr. Seuss, either personally or through his books. When I asked Pete Seeger to write one of these essays, he volunteered that he thought Dr. Seuss was one of the most important Americans of the twentieth century. We agree! Ted was always a little ahead of his time, and as we celebrate his 100th birthday four years into a new century, his place as an American icon is assured. What his books have to say about fairness, discrimination, peace, the environment, consumerism, and humanity in general is finding more advocates each year.

To help you form a better idea of the man behind the book, we've included a sampling of photos of him, advertisements and political cartoons that he did before he devoted his life to children's books, rough sketches and manuscripts from his books, and paintings and sculptures he created for his own amusement.

In gathering this material together we could not help but notice how connected all aspects of Ted's life were. Characters he first drew for humor magazines or political cartoons turned up decades later in his children's books. The architecture, flora and fauna, and sometimes the people he saw during his many travels to exotic lands also surfaced in his books.

TED AT A RECEPTION FOR HIM IN LA JOLLA, OCTOBER 1984.

Ted died on September 24, 1991. I was vacationing in France, and it was Cathy who called to break the news to me. We still miss him, but working on this book has brought us closer to him again. We hope you and your family will have as much pleasure reading it as we did compiling it.

—*Janet Schulman*
October 2004

THE VERY YOUNG TED

Toddler Ted (far left), circa 1906, all dressed up for this formal studio portrait. Ted (near left), circa 1910, with Theophrastus, his childhood toy dog, which remained with him long after he left home.

BY THE SEA

Every summer the Geisel family rented a cottage on a Long Island Sound beach near Clinton, Connecticut. Pictured (near right) are Theodor Robert Geisel with his children, Ted and Marnie, who was two years older than her brother, circa 1907. Ted (far right) proudly displays two fish that didn't get away, circa 1916.

THE WITTY BOY

Voted Class Artist and Class Wit by his high school classmates, Ted won the same reputation as class funnyman at Dartmouth. Pictured here with some of his college classmates, he is the second from the left on the first step.

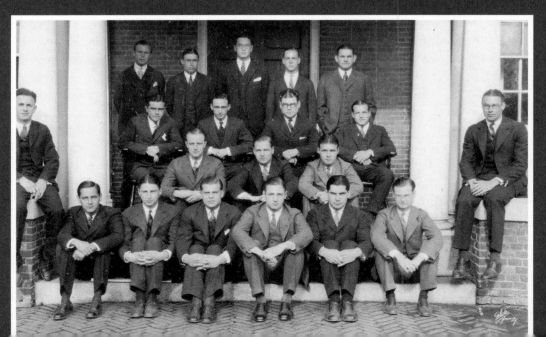

REPORTING FOR DUTY

Captain Theodor S. Geisel (left) during World War II, when he made army training films with Chuck Jones, creator of Road Runner and Wile E. Coyote. They became lifelong friends.

ON TOP OF THE WORLD

Ted (above) in Switzerland, the summer of 1926, after a brief fling with academic life at Oxford University.

TIME-OUT TO READ

Ted (right) in 1953 with the child star of The 5000 Fingers of Dr. T, the full-length feature film that Ted wrote.

TED AND HELEN

Ted in 1953 with his first wife, Helen Palmer. They met at Oxford and were married for nearly forty years when Helen died in 1967.

A ZOO OF HIS OWN

Ted and his "taxidermy" menagerie in his New York City apartment, 1937. For more examples of his animal sculptures, see page 83.

TED AND AUDREY

Ted with his second wife, Audrey Stone Dimond, in raccoon coats on the Cat in the Hat float in the Thanksgiving Day Parade in Detroit, 1979.

SEUSSIAN SARTORIAL SPLENDOR

After the 1950s, Ted, pictured here in 1978, always wore an elegant bow tie. "You can't dribble on bow ties," he once said.

he is everybody's inner child

Theodor Seuss Geisel—the indelible Dr. Seuss—set out to liberate children's imaginations from adult shackles and, in short order, won a following among rebellious spirits of all ages.

The commotion began, of course, on Mulberry Street. Young Marco, urged by his father to keep his "eyelids up," sees only an ordinary horse and wagon on his way home from school and, as a story, that alone will never do. Let the horse be a zebra, then; let the wagon be a chariot, the driver a charioteer. No—"a reindeer is better" . . . pulling "a fancy sled." And so it goes, in wilder and wilder, more and more stupendous imaginings, to the infectious da da *da* da de *dum* beat of a clamoring, cascading procession on Mulberry Street.

But such a story, Marco knows, is one that his stern, stick-to-the-facts father will never believe. Better keep it a secret between himself and the reader.

Far from being outraged by the indictment of adult obtuseness, the overseers of children's books were charmed. Here was an answer to the popularity of tacky comic strips, on the one hand, and the encroachment of here-and-now factuality (as opposed to, say, "The Three Bears"), on the other. Luminaries of the children's book world, headed by the redoubtable Anne Carroll Moore of the New York Public Library, were quick to give Marco's flight of fancy their blessing. The illustrations for *Mulberry Street*, Moore pointedly wrote, had "the dynamic quality of the comic strip."

Dr. Seuss was already well known, and much appreciated, as the creator of ads for the insecticide Flit, featuring an acrobatic, loose-limbed fellow named Henry (think Cat in the Hat) who takes deadly aim— "Quick, Henry, the Flit!"—at an assortment of improbable insects. Earlier, his outlandish animals had appeared in the old, old *Life* and in other humor magazines. When *Mulberry Street* came out, he had the backing of booksellers as well as the endorsement of experts.

Mulberry Street met no resistance, in any case, because grown-ups identify with Marco too. In his daydreams, in his tall tales, he is everybody's inner child—a reminder of how it felt to be a fantasizing nine- or ten-year-old.

From *Horton Hatches the Egg* onward, Dr. Seuss leaves the rest of us in the dust. The charioteers and brass bands and motorcycle cops that Marco dreams up could have sprung from the imagination of almost any American boy of the 1930s. Not so the Elephant-Bird that zooms from the egg that faithful Horton hatches for Mayzie, the no-good lazy bird with—*yes!*— "EARS AND A TAIL AND A TRUNK JUST LIKE HIS!" Nor the Fizza-ma-Wizza-ma-Dill or the Obsk, the Sneetches or the Grinch, of Seussian bestiary fame— successors to the Sidehill Dodger, the Hoop Snake, the Jackalope, and other fabulous critters of American comic legend.

Marco himself makes a triumphant return. The boy once enjoined by his stuffy father to "stop turning minnows into whales" waits hopefully for "a whole herd of whales" to surface in *McElligot's Pool*.

BARBARA BADER

author of *American Picturebooks from Noah's Ark to the Beast Within* and former editor of *Kirkus Reviews*

and to think
that i
saw it on
mulberry street

[ORIGINALLY PUBLISHED IN 1937]

When I leave home to walk to school,
Dad always says to me,
"Marco, keep your eyelids up
And see what you can see."

But when I tell him where I've been
And what I think I've seen,
He looks at me and sternly says,
"Your eyesight's much too keen.

"Stop telling such outlandish tales.
Stop turning minnows into whales."

Now, what can I say
When I get home today?

All the long way to school
And all the way back,
I've looked and I've looked
And I've kept careful track,
But all that I've noticed,
Except my own feet,
Was a horse and a wagon
On Mulberry Street.

That's nothing to tell of,
That won't do, of course . . .
Just a broken-down wagon
That's drawn by a horse.

That *can't* be my story. That's only a *start*.
I'll say that a ZEBRA was pulling that cart!
And that is a story that no one can beat,
When I say that I saw it on Mulberry Street.

Yes, the zebra is fine,
But I think it's a shame,
Such a marvelous beast
With a cart that's so tame.
The story would really be better to hear
If the driver I saw were a charioteer.
A gold and blue chariot's *something* to meet,
Rumbling like thunder down Mulberry Street!

No, it won't do at all . . .
A zebra's too small.

A reindeer is better;
He's fast and he's fleet,
And he'd look mighty smart
On old Mulberry Street.

Hold on a minute!
There's something wrong!
A reindeer hates the way it feels
To pull a thing that runs on wheels.

He'd be much happier, instead,
If he could pull a fancy sled.

Hmmmm . . . A reindeer and sleigh . . .
Say—*any*one could think of *that*,
Jack or Fred or Joe or Nat—
Say, even Jane could think of *that*.

But it isn't too late to make one little change.
A sleigh and an ELEPHANT! *There's* something strange!

I'll pick one with plenty of power and size,
A blue one with plenty of fun in his eyes.
And then, just to give him a little more tone,
Have a Rajah, with rubies, perched high on a throne.

Say! That makes a story that *no one* can beat,
When I say that I saw it on Mulberry Street.

But now I don't know . . .
It still doesn't seem right.

An elephant pulling a thing that's so light
Would whip it around in the air like a kite.

But he'd look simply grand
With a great big brass band!

A band that's so good should have someone to hear it,
But it's going so fast that it's hard to keep near it.
I'll put on a trailer! I know they won't mind
If a man sits and listens while hitched on behind.

But now is it fair? Is it fair what I've done?
I'll bet those wagons weigh more than a ton.
That's really too heavy a load for *one* beast;
I'll give him some helpers. He needs two, at least.

But now what worries me is this . . .
Mulberry Street runs into Bliss,

Unless there's something I can fix up,
There'll be an *awful* traffic mix-up!

16

It takes Police to do the trick,
To guide them through where traffic's thick—
It takes Police to do the trick.
They'll never crash now. They'll race at top speed
With Sergeant Mulvaney, himself, in the lead.

The Mayor is there
And he thinks it is grand,
And he raises his hat
As they dash by the stand.

The Mayor is there
And the Aldermen too,
All waving big banners
Of red, white and blue.

And that is a story that NO ONE can beat
When I say that I saw it on Mulberry Street!

With a roar of its motor an airplane appears
And dumps out confetti while everyone cheers.

And that makes a story that's really not bad!
But it still could be better. Suppose that I add . . . .

19

. . . A Chinese man
Who eats with sticks . . .

A big Magician
Doing tricks . . .

A ten-foot beard
That needs a comb . . .

No time for more,
I'm almost home.

I swung 'round the corner
And dashed through the gate,
I ran up the steps
And I felt simply GREAT!

FOR I HAD A STORY THAT NO ONE COULD BEAT!
AND TO THINK THAT I SAW IT ON MULBERRY STREET!

But Dad said quite calmly,
"Just draw up your stool
And tell me the sights
On the way home from school."

There was so much to tell, I JUST COULDN'T BEGIN!
Dad looked at me sharply and pulled at his chin.
He frowned at me sternly from there in his seat,
"Was there nothing to look at . . . no people to greet?
Did *nothing* excite you or make your heart beat?"

"Nothing," I said, growing red as a beet,
"But a plain horse and wagon on Mulberry Street."

Toddler Ted circa 1906.

IT ALL STARTED IN SPRINGFIELD

Ted Geisel grew up at 74 Fairfield Street in Springfield, Massachusetts, shown above in a contemporary photo. It was his home from age four until he left for Dartmouth College. During his childhood, horse-drawn wagons, like those in the vintage postcard below, were ubiquitous. He surely saw them on Mulberry Street—yes, there really is a Mulberry Street in Springfield, but it doesn't cross Bliss and it never saw the zany wagons pictured in Dr. Seuss's first children's book.

Ted at his drawing board with the Cat in the Hat. This sculpture, by Ted's stepdaughter Lark Dimond-Cates, is the centerpiece of the Dr. Seuss National Memorial Sculpture Garden at the Quadrangle in Springfield, Massachusetts.

SPRINGFIELD, MASS. MAIN STREET ARCH.

you're never too old

"Seuss? Seuss? Dr. Seuss?" The name had a distant ring. We had asked our four-year-old son, Leo, if there was anything special he wanted for Christmas, and he said, yes, a book called *McElligot's Pool* by Dr. Seuss. His teacher at the Oak Lane Day School had read it to his class. "It was about this kid who went fishing in this little pool," said Leo, "and guess what? . . ."

Bypassing Leo's bright-eyed eagerness to tell "what," Stan, in his best Papa Bear often-wrong-but-never-in-doubt mode, said, "Son, there's no such name as McElligot. It must be McElliot. Tell you what, why don't you ask the teacher to write the name of the book and the author on a piece of paper and we'll consult Santa Claus about it." The next day, Leo handed us a paper that said, "*McElligot's Pool* by Dr. Seuss."

What rang that distant bell was the recollection from our own childhood of a ubiquitous advertising campaign for a household insecticide called Flit. The ads depicted two characters stalking an enormous mosquito. "Quick, Henry, the Flit!" urged one of the characters. The ads were signed "Dr. Seuss."

McElligot's Pool turned out to be a wonderfully imaginative story—beautifully painted, beautifully designed, and delightfully rhymed. It told the story of a boy who drops a hopeful hook into a tiny pool that just may be connected to every stream, river, lake, and ocean of the world. The piscatorial possibilities are endless. We see sea creatures of every shape and size in McElligot's Pool and its tributaries.

Some years after Leo introduced us to Dr. Seuss, it was our great good fortune to be edited and published by Dr. Seuss. In fact, he virtually godfathered our Berenstain Bears into being.

We took Leo's old copy of *McElligot's Pool* to our first meeting with Dr. Seuss for autographing. Ted, as we were immediately instructed to call him, autographed the book: "For Leo, who is now too old for this book—Dr. Seuss."

Ted was wrong; nobody is ever too old for Dr. Seuss.

STAN AND JAN BERENSTAIN

creators of the Berenstain Bears

mcelligot's pool

[ORIGINALLY PUBLISHED IN 1947]

"Young man," laughed the farmer,
"You're sort of a fool!
You'll *never* catch fish
In McElligot's Pool!

"The pool is too small.
And, you might as well know it,
When people have junk
Here's the place that they throw it.

"You might catch a boot
Or you might catch a can.
You might catch a bottle,
But listen, young man . . .
If you sat fifty years
With your worms and your wishes,
You'd grow a long beard
Long before you'd catch fishes!"

"Hmmm . . ." answered Marco,
"It *may* be you're right.
I've been here three hours
Without one single bite.
There *might* be no fish . . .

   ". . . But, again,
   Well, there *might!*

"'Cause you never can tell
What goes on down below!

   "This pool *might* be bigger
   Than you or I know!"

This MIGHT be a pool, like I've read of in books,
Connected to one of those underground brooks!

An underground river that starts here and flows
Right under the pasture! And then . . . well, *who knows?*

It *might* go along, down where no one can see,
Right under State Highway Two-Hundred-and-Three!
Right under the wagons! Right under the toes
Of Mrs. Umbroso who's hanging out clothes!

It *might* keep on flowing . . . perhaps . . . who can tell? . . .
Right under the people in Sneeden's Hotel!
Right under the grass where they're playing croquet!
Then under the mountains and far, far away!

This *might* be a river,
Now mightn't it be,

Connecting
        McElligot's Pool
            With the sea!

Then maybe some fish might be swimming toward me!

(If such a thing *could* be,
They certainly *would* be!)

Some very smart fellow might point out the way
To the place where I'm fishing. And that's why I say
If I wait long enough; if I'm patient and cool,
Who knows *what* I'll catch in McElligot's Pool!

I might catch a thin fish,

I might catch a stout fish.

I might catch a short

or
a
long,
long
drawn-out fish!

34

Any kind! Any shape! Any color or size!
I *might* catch some fish that would open your eyes!

I won't be surprised if a *Dog Fish* appears!
Complete with a collar and long floppy ears!
Whoofing along! And perhaps he might chase
A whole lot of *Catfish* right straight to this place!

I might catch a fish
With a pinwheel-like tail!

I might catch a fish
Who has fins like a sail!

I might catch some young fish
Some high-jumping friskers.

I might catch an old one
With long flowing whiskers!

I might catch a fish
With a long curly nose.

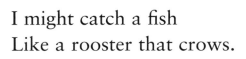

I might catch a fish
Like a rooster that crows.

I might catch a fish
With a checkerboard belly,

Or even a fish
Made of strawberry jelly!

I might catch a Sea Horse.
(Now mightn't I now . . . ?)

I might catch a fish
Who is partly a cow!

Some fish from the Tropics, all sunburned and hot,
Might decide to swim up!
       Well they might . . .
       Might they not?
Racing up north for a chance to get cool,
Full steam ahead for McElligot's Pool!

Some Eskimo Fish
From beyond Hudson Bay
Might decide to swim down;
Might be headed this way!

It's a pretty long trip,
But they *might*
And they *may*.

I might catch an eel . . .
(Well, I might. It depends.)
. . . A long twisting eel
With a lot of strange bends
And, oddly enough,
With a head on both ends!

One doesn't catch *this* kind of fish as a rule,
But the chances are fine in McElligot's Pool!

I might catch a fish
With a terrible grouch . . .

Or an Australian fish
With a kangaroo's pouch!

Who wants to catch small ones like mackerel or trout!
SAY! I'll catch a Saw Fish with such a long snout
That he needs an assistant to help him about!

If I wait long enough, if I'm patient and cool,
Who knows *what* I'll catch in McElligot's Pool!

Some rough-neck old Lobster,
All gristle and muscle,
Might grab at my bait,
Then would I have a tussle!

To land one so tough might
    take two or three hours,
But the *next* might be easy . . .

. . . The kind that likes flowers.

I *might* catch some sort of a fast-moving bloke
Who zips through the waves with an over-arm stroke!

(I *might* and I *may* and that's really no joke!)

A fish even faster!
A fish, if you please,
Who slides down the sides
Of strange islands on skis!

He *might* ski on over and pay me a visit.
That's not impossible . . . really, now is it?

Some Circus Fish!
Fish from an acrobat school,
Might stage a big show in McElligot's Pool!

Or I might catch a fish
From a stranger place yet!
From the world's highest river
In far-off Tibet,
Where the falls are so steep
That it's dangerous to ride 'em,
So the fish put up chutes
And they float down beside 'em.

From the world's deepest ocean,
From way down below,
From down in the mud where the deep-divers go,
From down in the mire and the muck and the murk,
I might catch some fish who are all going, "GLURK!"

WHALES!
I'll catch whales!
Yes, a whole herd of whales!
All spouting their spouts
And all thrashing their tails!

I'll catch fifty whales,
Then I'll stop for the day
'Cause there's *nothing* that's bigger
Than whales, so they say.

Still, of course,
It *might* be . . .

. . . that there IS something bigger!
Some sort of a kind of
A THING-A-MA-JIGGER!!

A fish that's so big, if you know what I mean,
That he makes a whale look like a tiny sardine!

Oh, the sea is so full of a number of fish,
If a fellow is patient, he *might* get his wish!

And that's why I think
That I'm not such a fool
When I sit here and fish
In McElligot's Pool!

Yellow fish (top and bottom) and turtle (below) from *One Fish Two Fish Red Fish Blue Fish,* 1960.

SECRETS OF THE DEEP Vol. II

By Old Captain Taylor

•

Aquatints by Dr. Seuss

THE SEUSS NAVY

More than a decade before Ted Geisel dreamed up the fabulous fishy world of McElligot's Pool, *his aquatic mutations were happily selling Essomarine motor oil. Ted's ads and the booklet* Secrets of the Deep *were such a hit for Essomarine that it launched a Seuss Navy at the National Motor Boat Show in New York City in 1936. Admiral-in-Chief Dr. Seuss designed an amusing certificate of commission and in later years funny drinking glasses and an ashtray. He also produced a real showstopper: a six-act comedy,* Little Dramas of the Deep. *Ted retired from his navy in 1941, but Essomarine continued to enjoy the benefits of the fun he brought to its promotions.*

Red and blue creatures, pictured here, from *Secrets of the Deep.*

From *Hop on Pop,* 1962.

thank you, mcgrew

I had a wonderful time today. For the first time in years, I reread the early Dr. Seuss classic *If I Ran the Zoo*. Its copyright informed me that this book came out in 1950, which means my parents first read it to me when I was about five years old. Today, I was five years old all over again.

Page by page, everything came back. There was young Gerald McGrew, dressed in striped pants, a red necktie, and a zookeeper's hat, standing outside a lion's cage. And there were all those loopy animals: the Joat, the Lunk, the Thwerll, the Chugg, and the Fizza-ma-Wizza-ma-Dill. Once again I savored the bizarre names of their far-flung habitats: the Desert of Zind, the Island of Gwark, Zomba-ma-Tant, and Motta-fa-Potta-fa-Pell. Every one of Dr. Seuss's illustrations sprung from the page, long forgotten and suddenly, vividly remembered.

Millions of us, of all ages, have these memories in common. Gerald McGrew connects us to each other, as do Horton, Thidwick, Yertle, McElligot, and Bartholomew Cubbins. For many of us, Dr. Seuss's rhymes and wacky wordplay were our first experience of metrical verse, verbal gymnastics, and unbridled literary imagination. And we rediscovered all these unique qualities when we introduced his books to our own kids.

But the spirit of Dr. Seuss hovers over me in another way, too. A few years ago, I began writing children's picture books myself. The first was *The Remarkable Farkle McBride,* and four others have followed. They are written in meticulous verse; they make use of nutty, far-fetched rhymes; they feature anthropomorphic animals. And just look at the character names! Surely Farkle McBride and Gerald McGrew are first cousins. Reading Dr. Seuss today forces me to acknowledge the enormous debt I owe this genial man. His verses have indelibly marked my children's-book-writing DNA. More simply put, I unwittingly rip him off.

Today, as I read *If I Ran the Zoo,* a question floated into my mind again and again: If Dr. Seuss had not written his, would I ever have written mine? I wonder how many hundreds of children's book authors over the last fifty years have asked themselves the same question.

JOHN LITHGOW

actor and children's book author

if i ran the zoo

[ORIGINALLY PUBLISHED IN 1950]

"It's a pretty good zoo,"
Said young Gerald McGrew,
"And the fellow who runs it
Seems proud of it, too."

"But if *I* ran the zoo,"
Said young Gerald McGrew,
"I'd make a few changes.
That's just what I'd do ..."

The lions and tigers and that kind of stuff
They have up here now are not *quite* good enough.
You see things like these in just any old zoo.
They're awfully old-fashioned. I want something *new*!

So I'd open each cage. I'd unlock every pen,
Let the animals go, and start over again.
And, somehow or other, I think I could find
Some beasts of a much more un-usual kind.

A *four*-footed lion's not much of a beast.
The one in my zoo will have *ten* feet, at least!
Five legs on the left and five more on the right.
Then people will stare and they'll say, "What a sight!
This Zoo Keeper, New Keeper Gerald's quite keen.
That's the gol-darndest lion I ever have seen!"

My New Zoo, McGrew Zoo, will make people talk.
My New Zoo, McGrew Zoo, will make people gawk
At the strangest odd creatures that ever did walk.
I'll get, for my zoo, a new sort-of-a-hen
Who roosts in another hen's topknot, and *then*
Another one roosts in the topknot of his,
And another in *his,* and another in HIS,
And so forth and upward and onward, gee whizz!

But that's just a start. I'll do better than *that*.
They'll see me next day, in my zoo-keeper's hat,
Coming into my zoo with an Elephant-Cat!

They'll be so surprised they'll all swallow their gum.
They'll ask, when they see my strange animals come,
"Where *do* you suppose he gets things like that from?
His animals all have such very odd faces.
I'll bet he must hunt them in rather odd places!"

63

And that's what I'll do,
Said young Gerald McGrew.
If you want to catch beasts you don't see every day,
You have to go places quite out-of-the-way.
You have to go places no others can get to.
You have to get cold and you have to get wet, too.
Up past the North Pole, where the frozen winds squeal,
I'll go and I'll hunt in my Skeegle-mobile
And bring back a family of *What-do-you-know!*
And that's how my New Zoo, McGrew Zoo, will grow.

I'll hunt in the mountains of Zomba-ma-Tant
With helpers who all wear their eyes at a slant,
And capture a fine fluffy bird called the Bustard
Who only eats custard with sauce made of mustard.
And, also, a very fine beast called the Flustard
Who only eats mustard with sauce made of custard.

I'll catch 'em in caves and I'll catch 'em in brooks,
I'll catch 'em in crannies, I'll catch 'em in nooks
That you don't read about in geography books.

I'll catch 'em in countries that no one can spell
Like the country of Motta-fa-Potta-fa-Pell.
In a country like that, if a hunter is clever,
He'll hunt up some beasts that you never saw ever!

I'll load up five boats with a family of Joats
Whose feet are like cows', but wear squirrel-skin coats
And sit down like dogs, but have voices like goats—
Excepting they can't sing the very high notes.

And then I'll go down to the Wilds of Nantucket
And capture a family of Lunks in a bucket.
Then people will say, "Now I like that boy heaps.
His New Zoo, McGrew Zoo, is growing by leaps.
He captures them wild and he captures them meek,
He captures them slim and he captures them sleek.
What *do* you suppose he will capture next week?"

I'll capture one tiny. I'll capture one cute.
I'll capture a deer that no hunter would shoot.
A deer that's so nice he could sleep in your bed
If it weren't for those horns that he has on his head.

And speaking of horns that are just a bit queer,
I'll bring back a very odd family of deer:
A father, a mother, two sisters, a brother
Whose horns are connected, from one to the other,
Whose horns are so mixed they can't tell them apart,
Can't tell where they end and can't tell where they start!
Each deer's mighty puzzled. He's never yet found
If *his* horns are *hers,* or the other way 'round.

I'll capture them fat and I'll capture them scrawny.
I'll capture a scraggle-foot Mulligatawny,
A high-stepping animal fast as the wind
From the blistering sands of the Desert of Zind.
This beast is the beast that the brave chieftains ride
When they want to go fast to find some place to hide.
A Mulligatawny is fine for my zoo
And so is a chieftain. I'll bring one back, too.

In the Far Western part
Of south-east North Dakota
Lives a very fine animal
Called the Iota.
But I'll capture one
Who is even much finer
In the north-eastern west part
Of South Carolina.

When people see *him*, they will say, "Now, by thunder!
This New Zoo, McGrew Zoo, is really a wonder!"

Most beasts are quite friendly, but still, in some lands
Some beasts are too dangerous to catch with bare hands.
For those that are ugly and vicious and mean
I'll build a Bad-Animal-Catching-Machine.
It's rather expensive to build such a kit,
But with it a hunter can never get bit.

A zoo should have bugs, so I'll capture a Thwerll.
Whose legs are snarled up in a terrible snerl.

And then I'll go out and I'll capture some Chuggs,
Some keen-shooter, mean-shooter, bean-shooter bugs.

I'll go to the African island of Yerka
And bring back a tizzle-topped Tufted Mazurka,
A kind of canary with quite a tall throat.
His neck is so long, if he swallows an oat
For breakfast the first day of April, they say
It has to go down such a very long way
That it gets to his stomach the fifteenth of May.

I'll bag a big bug
Who is very surprising,
A feller who has
A propeller for rising
And zooming around
Making cross-country hops,
From Texas to Boston
With only two stops.
Now *that* sort of thing
For a bug is just tops!

And when I've caught *him*,
Then the next thing you know
I'll go and I'll capture
A wild Tick-Tack-Toe,
With X's that win
And with Zeros that lose.
He'll look mighty good
In this Zoo of McGrew's.

I'll bring back a Gusset, a Gherkin, a Gasket
And also a Gootch from the wilds of Nantasket.

And eight Persian Princes will carry the basket,
But what *their* names are, I don't know. So don't ask it.

In a cave in Kartoom lives a beast called the Natch
That no other hunter's been able to catch.
He's hidden for years in his cave with a pout
And no one's been able to make him come out.
But *I'll* coax him out with a wonderful meal
That's cooked by my cooks in my Cooker-mobile.

They'll fix up a dish that is just to his taste;
Three chicken croquettes made of library paste,
Then sprinkled with peanut shucks, pickled and spiced,
Then baked at 600 degrees and then iced.
It's mighty hard cooking to cook up such feasts
But that's how the New Zoo, McGrew Zoo, gets beasts.

I'll go to the far-away Mountains of Tobsk
Near the River of Nobsk, and I'll bring back an Obsk,
A sort of a kind of a Thing-a-ma-Bobsk
Who only eats rhubarb and corn-on-the-cobsk.
Then people will flock to my zoo in a mobsk.
"McGrew," they will say, "does a wonderful jobsk!
He hunts with such vim and he hunts with such vigor,
His New Zoo, McGrew Zoo, gets bigger and bigger!"

And, speaking of birds, there's the Russian Palooski,
Whose headski is redski and belly is blueski.
I'll get one of *them* for my Zooski McGrewski.

Then the whole town will gasp, "Why, this boy never sleeps!
No keeper before ever kept what *he* keeps!
There's no telling WHAT that young fellow will do!"
And then, just to show them, I'll sail to Ka-Troo
And
    Bring
       Back

an IT-KUTCH

a PREEP

a NERKLE

and a PROO

a NERD

and a SEERSUCKER, too!

I'll hunt in the Jungles of Hippo-no-Hungus
And bring back a flock of wild Bippo-no-Bungus!
The Bippo-no-Bungus from Hippo-no-Hungus
Are better than those down in Dippo-no-Dungus
And smarter than those out in Nippo-no-Nungus.
And that's why I'll catch 'em in Hippo-no-Hungus
Instead of those others in Nungus and Dungus.
And people will say when they see these Bips bounding,
"This Zoo Keeper, New Keeper's simply astounding!
He travels so far that you'd think he would drop!
When *do* you suppose this young fellow will stop?"

Stop . . . ?
Well, I should.
But I won't stop until
I've captured the Fizza-ma-Wizza-ma-Dill,
The world's biggest bird from the Island of Gwark
Who only eats pine trees and spits out the bark.
And boy! When I get *him* back home to my park,
The whole *world* will say, "Young McGrew's made his mark.
He's built a zoo better than Noah's whole Ark!
These wonderful, marvelous beasts that he chooses
Have made him the greatest of all the McGrewses!"

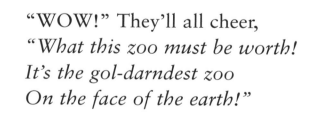

"WOW!" They'll all cheer,
"What this zoo *must be worth!*
It's the gol-darndest zoo
On the face of the earth!"

"Yes . . .
That's what I'd do,"
Said young Gerald McGrew.
"I'd make a few changes
If *I* ran the zoo."

"SEMI-NORMAL
GREEN-LIDDED
FAWN"

"TWO-HORNED
DROUBERHANNUS"

"ANTHONY
DREXEL
GOLDFARB"

"MULBERRY
STREET
UNICORN"

"ANDULOVIAN
GRACKLER"

"BLUE-GREEN
ABELARD"

ANIMALS THAT NEVER WERE

Not only did Ted Geisel draw animals that were, well, a bit different, he also created sculptures that combine elements from real animals with elements from his fertile imagination. His father, who actually ran the zoo in Springfield, Massachusetts, for thirty years, supplied him with the elk antlers (top left), the gazelle (top right) and African antelope (bottom right) horns, the toucan beak, and the rhinoceros horn transformed into a unicorn that you see here. "Anthony Drexel Goldfarb" has floppy, rabbit-like ears of leather, and we're not sure if he is intended to be man or beast. The faces are made of plaster. All shown here were made in 1934 for his own amusement and hung in his home.

a gift worth waiting for

About a month after I was born, Ted Geisel sent his publisher, Bennett Cerf—who also happened to be my father—a letter offering him belated congratulations on my arrival. In the letter, Ted offered up a saga worthy of *And to Think That I Saw It on Mulberry Street* to explain why no gift for me had been attached. "So far we can't find the exactly appropriate present for a lad of his talents and lineage," he wrote. "It may take years, but tell him to wait." Ted was kidding, but the "presents" he did give me have not only provided me with a lifetime of reading enjoyment but have actually shaped my career.

Horton Hatches the Egg was the first book that I can remember my parents reading to me. I can still recall my dad explaining to me what a moral is, guaranteeing that the lines "I meant what I said and I said what I meant. . . . An elephant's faithful one hundred per cent!" would become permanently etched in my memory. My father also pointed out that Horton's adventures sitting atop the egg of the irresponsible Mayzie proved that it was possible to combine humor with a serious message.

I'll always treasure the excitement of my dad's bringing home—hot off the press—*McElligot's Pool*. But the biggest thrill of all came when my first literary hero, Horton, returned to our home as the star of a new Seuss morality tale, *Horton Hears a Who!* Again, there was an unforgettable Seussian adage: "A person's a person, no matter how small." The book embodies a principle that defines all of Ted Geisel's work: that children be given all the care and respect that authors usually reserve only for their fellow grown-ups.

Within three years, Ted had proven his own point with perhaps his most significant contribution to children's literature, *The Cat in the Hat*. Using just 223 different words from a first-grade vocabulary list, he made learning to read fun. Building on that book's success, my mother, Phyllis Cerf Wagner, and Ted launched Beginner Books. Some years later, Beginner Books gave me my first job out of college. There I saw firsthand how Ted made magic with a handful of words and an untethered imagination.

It could be argued that if Ted hadn't created *The Cat in the Hat,* then *Sesame Street,* with its own unique mix of serious education and inspired nonsense, would never have been conceived. During its first year on the air, *Sesame Street* gave me my second post-college job, and I've spent the better part of the last four decades writing and producing music, lyrics, scripts, recordings, and other bits of curriculum-based insanity for the show.

Recently Michael Frith, Dr. Seuss's longtime editor, and I helped create *Between the Lions* for PBS. We brought to the show many Seussian techniques to help kids learn to read and also a bit of his name: Theo, the father lion in the show.

A copy of the letter Ted sent my father back in 1941 still hangs by a window overlooking my garden, where every day, "from sun in the summer" to "rain when it's fall-ish" (to quote another memorable line from *Horton Hears a Who!*), it reminds me of the promise Ted Geisel made in jest but that, in reality, has been many, many times fulfilled.

CHRISTOPHER CERF
writer, composer, and television producer

horton
hears
a who!

[ORIGINALLY PUBLISHED IN 1954]

On the fifteenth of May, in the Jungle of Nool,
In the heat of the day, in the cool of the pool,
He was splashing...enjoying the jungle's great joys...
When Horton the elephant heard a small noise.

So Horton stopped splashing. He looked toward the sound.
"That's funny," thought Horton. "There's no one around."
Then he heard it again! Just a very faint yelp
As if some tiny person were calling for help.
"I'll help you," said Horton. "But *who* are you? *Where?*"
He looked and he looked. He could see nothing there
But a small speck of dust blowing past through the air.

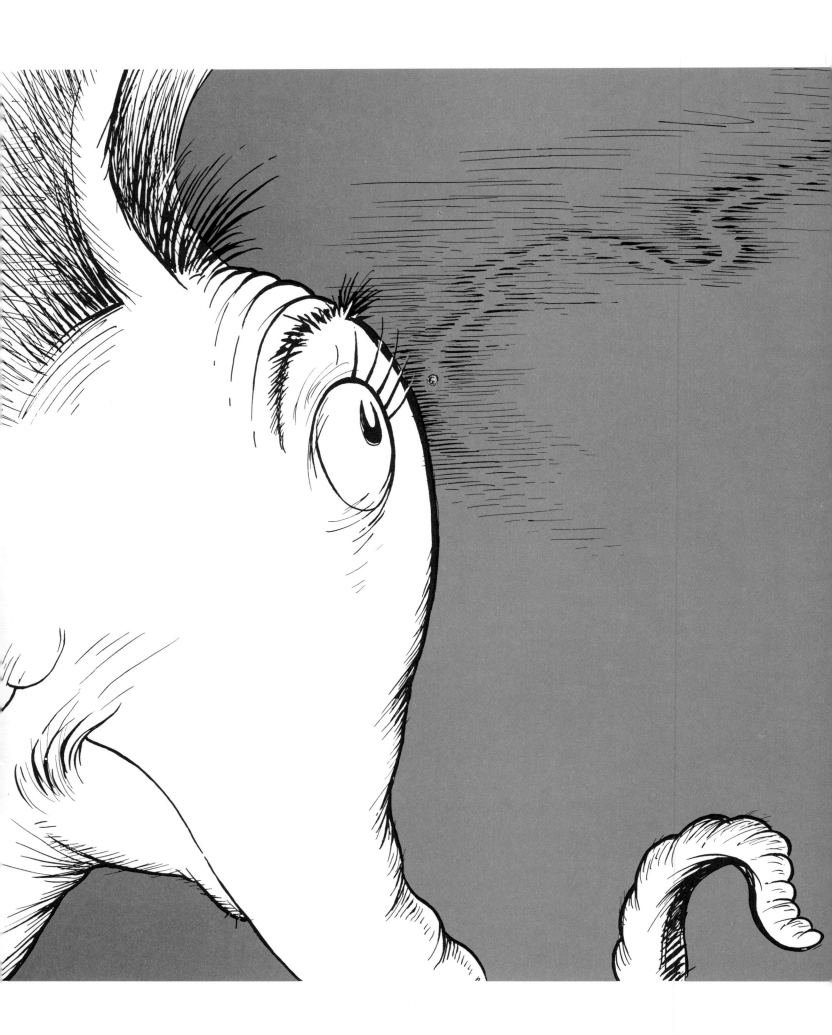

"I say!" murmured Horton. "I've never heard tell
Of a small speck of dust that is able to yell.
So you know what I think?... Why, I think that there must
Be someone on top of that small speck of dust!
Some sort of a creature of *very* small size,
Too small to be seen by an elephant's eyes...

"... some poor little person who's shaking with fear
That he'll blow in the pool! He has no way to steer!
I'll just have to save him. Because, after all,
A person's a person, no matter how small."

So, gently, and using the greatest of care,
The elephant stretched his great trunk through the air,
And he lifted the dust speck and carried it over
And placed it down, safe, on a very soft clover.

"Humpf!" humpfed a voice. 'Twas a sour kangaroo.
And the young kangaroo in her pouch said "Humpf!" too.
"Why, that speck is as small as the head of a pin.
A person on *that?* . . . Why, there never has been!"

"Believe me," said Horton. "I tell you sincerely,
My ears are quite keen and I heard him quite clearly.
I *know* there's a person down there. And, what's more,
Quite likely there's two. Even three. Even four.
Quite likely . . .

" . . . a family, for all that we know!
A family with children just starting to grow.
So, please," Horton said, "as a favor to me,
Try not to disturb them. Just please let them be."

"I think you're a fool!" laughed the sour kangaroo
And the young kangaroo in her pouch said, "Me, too!
You're the biggest blame fool in the Jungle of Nool!"
And the kangaroos plunged in the cool of the pool.
"What terrible splashing!" the elephant frowned.
"I can't let my very small persons get drowned!
I've *got* to protect them. I'm bigger than they."
So he plucked up the clover and hustled away.

Through the high jungle tree tops, the news quickly spread:
"He talks to a dust speck! He's out of this head!
Just look at him walk with that speck on that flower!"
And Horton walked, worrying, almost an hour.
"Should I put this speck down? . . ." Horton thought with alarm.
"If I do, these small persons may come to great harm.
I *can't* put it down. And I *won't!* After all
A person's a person. No matter how small."

Then Horton stopped walking.
The speck-voice was talking!
The voice was so faint he could just barely hear it.
"Speak *up,* please," said Horton. He put his ear near it.

"My friend," came the voice, "you're a *very* fine friend.
You've helped all us folks on this dust speck no end.
You've saved all our houses, our ceilings and floors.
You've saved all our churches and grocery stores."

"You mean . . ." Horton gasped, "you have *buildings* there, *too?*"

"Oh, yes" piped the voice. "We most certainly do. . . .
"I know," called the voice, "I'm too small to be seen
But I'm Mayor of a town that is friendly and clean.
Our buildings, to you, would seem terribly small
But to us, who aren't big, they are wonderfully tall.
My town is called *Who*-ville, for I am a *Who*
And we *Whos* are all thankful and grateful to you."

And Horton called back to the Mayor of the town,
"You're safe now. Don't worry. I won't let you down."

But, just as he spoke to the Mayor of the speck,
Three big jungle monkeys climbed up Horton's neck!
The Wickersham Brothers came shouting, "What rot!
This elephant's talking to *Whos* who are *not!*
There *aren't* any *Whos!* And they *don't* have a Mayor!
And *we're* going to stop all this nonsense! *So there!*"

They snatched Horton's clover! They carried it off
To a black-bottomed eagle named Vlad Vlad-i-koff,
A mighty strong eagle, of very swift wing,
And they said, "Will you kindly get rid of this thing?"
And, before the poor elephant even could speak,
That eagle flew off with the flower in his beak.

All that late afternoon and far into the night
That black-bottomed bird flapped his wings in fast flight,
While Horton chased after, with groans, over stones
That tattered his toenails and battered his bones,
And begged, "Please don't harm all my little folks, who
Have as much right to live as us bigger folks do!"

But far, far beyond him, that eagle kept flapping
And over his shoulder called back, "Quit your yapping.
I'll fly the night through. I'm a bird. I don't mind it.
And I'll hide this, tomorrow, where *you'll* never find it!"

And at 6:56 the next morning he did it.
It sure was a terrible place that he hid it.
He let that small clover drop somewhere inside
Of a great patch of clovers a hundred miles wide!
"Find THAT!" sneered the bird. "But I think you will fail."
And he left
With a flip
Of his black-bottomed tail.

"I'll find it!" cried Horton. "I'll find it or bust!
I SHALL find my friends on my small speck of dust!"
And clover, by clover, by clover with care
He picked up and searched them, and called, "Are you there?"
But clover, by clover, by clover he found
That the one that he sought for was just not around.
And by noon poor old Horton, more dead than alive,
Had picked, searched, and piled up, nine thousand and five.

Then, on through the afternoon, hour after hour . . .
Till he found them at last! On the three millionth flower!
"My friends!" cried the elephant. "Tell me! Do tell!
Are you safe? Are you sound? Are you whole? Are you well?"

From down on the speck came the voice of the Mayor:

"We've *really* had trouble! Much more than our share.
When that black-bottomed birdie let go and we dropped,
We landed so hard that our clocks have all stopped.
Our tea-pots are broken. Our rocking-chairs smashed.
And our bicycle tires all blew up when we crashed.
So, Horton, *please!*" pleaded that voice of the Mayor's,
"Will you stick by us *Whos* while we're making repairs?"

"Of course," Horton answered. "Of course I will stick.
I'll stick by you small folks through thin and through thick!"

"Humpf!"
Humpfed a voice!
"For almost two days you've run wild and insisted
On chatting with persons who've never existed.
Such carryings-on in our peaceable jungle!
We've had quite enough of your bellowing bungle!
And I'm here to state," snapped the big kangaroo,
"That your silly nonsensical game is all through!"
And the young kangaroo in her pouch said, "Me, too!"

"With the help of the Wickersham Brothers and dozens
Of Wickersham Uncles and Wickersham Cousins
And Wickersham In-Laws, whose help I've engaged,
You're going to be roped! And you're going to be caged!
And, as for your dust speck . . . *hah! That* we shall boil
In a hot steaming kettle of Beezle-Nut oil!"

"*Boil* it? . . ." gasped Horton!
"Oh, that you *can't* do!
It's all full of persons!
They'll *prove* it to you!"

"Mr. Mayor! Mr. Mayor!" Horton called. "Mr. Mayor!
You've *got* to prove now that you really are there!
So call a big meeting. Get everyone out.
Make every *Who* holler! Make every *Who* shout!
Make every *Who* scream! If you don't, every *Who*
Is going to end up in a Beezle-Nut stew!"

And, down on the dust speck, the scared little Mayor
Quick called a big meeting in *Who*-ville Town Square.
And his people cried loudly. They cried out in fear:

"We are here! We are here! We are here! We are here!"

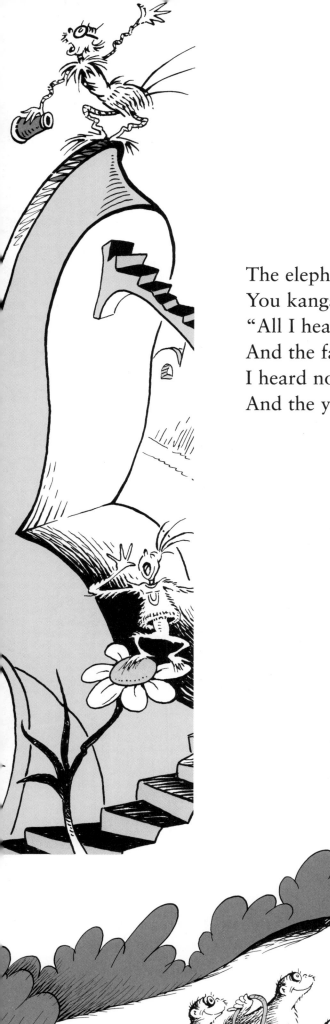

The elephant smiled: "That was clear as a bell.
You kangaroos surely heard *that* very well."
"All I heard," snapped the big kangaroo, "was the breeze,
And the faint sound of wind through the far-distant trees.
I heard no small voices. And you didn't either."
And the young kangaroo in her pouch said, "Me neither."

"Grab him!" they shouted. "And cage the big dope!
Lasso his stomach with ten miles of rope!
Tie the knots tight so he'll *never* shake loose!
Then dunk that dumb speck in the Beezle-Nut juice!"

Horton fought back with great vigor and vim
But the Wickersham gang was too many for him.
They beat him! They mauled him! They started to haul
Him into his cage! But he managed to call
To the Mayor: "Don't give up! I believe in you all!
A person's a person, no matter how small!
And you very small persons will *not* have to die
If you make yourselves heard! *So come on, now, and TRY!*"

The Mayor grabbed a tom-tom. He started to smack it.
And, all over *Who*-ville, they whooped up a racket.
They rattled tin kettles! They beat on brass pans,
On garbage pail tops and old cranberry cans!
They blew on bazookas and blasted great toots
On clarinets, oom-pahs and boom-pahs and flutes!

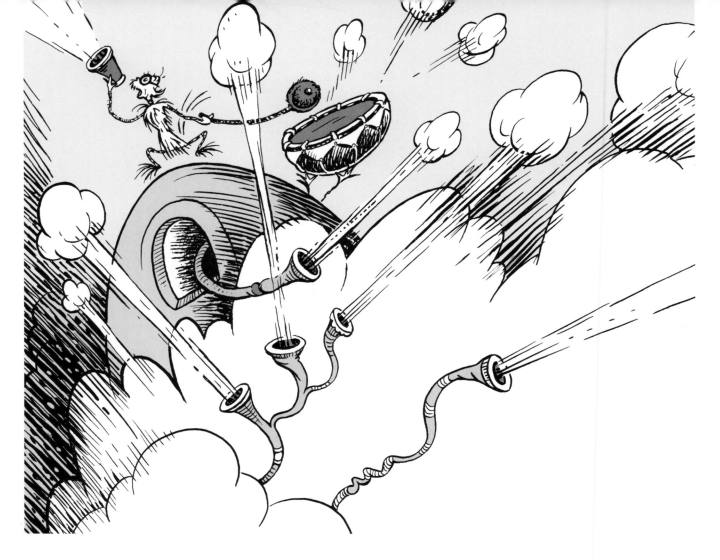

Great gusts of loud racket rang high through the air.
They rattled and shook the whole sky! And the Mayor
Called up through the howling mad hullabaloo:

"Hey, Horton! *How's this?* Is our sound coming through?"

And Horton called back, "I can hear you just fine.
But the kangaroos' ears aren't as strong, quite, as mine.
They don't hear a thing! Are you *sure* all your boys
Are doing their best? Are they ALL making noise?
Are you sure every *Who* down in *Who*-ville is working?
Quick! Look through your town! Is there anyone shirking?"

Through the town rushed the Mayor, from the east to the west.
But *every*one seemed to be doing his best.
*Every*one seemed to be yapping or yipping!
*Every*one seemed to be beeping or bipping!
But it *wasn't enough,* all this ruckus and roar!
He HAD to find someone to help him make more.
He raced through each building! He searched floor-to-floor!

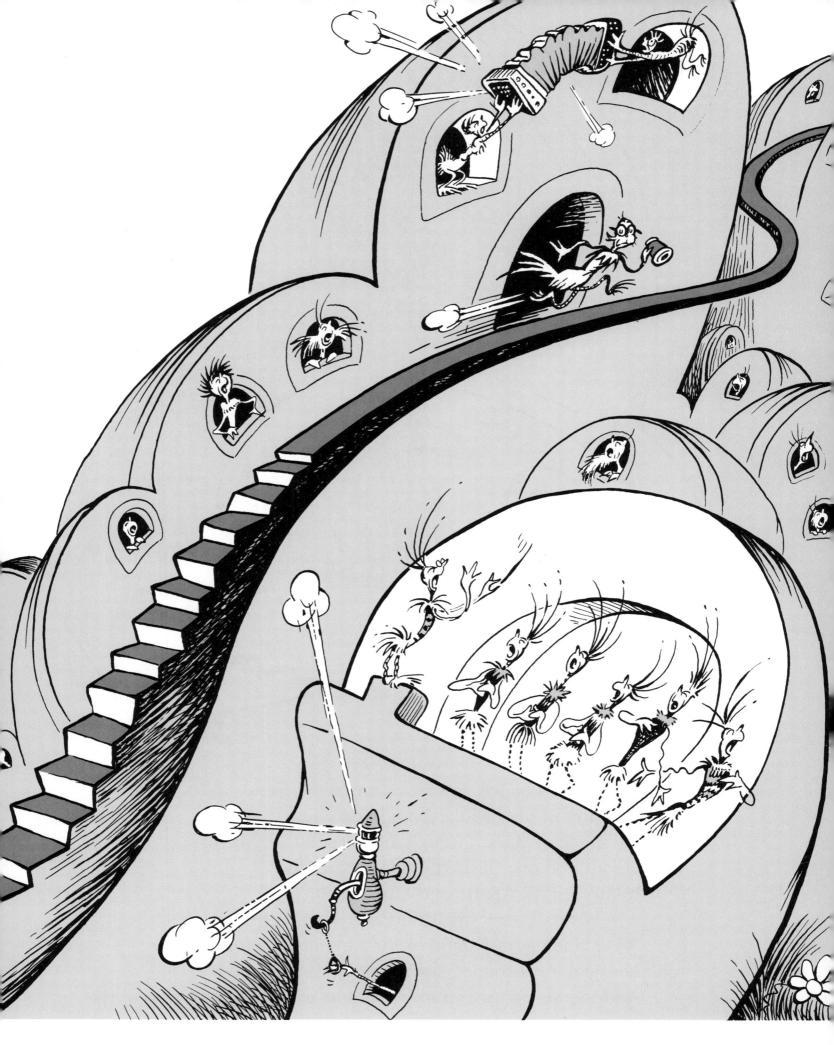

111

And, just as he felt he was getting nowhere,
And almost about to give up in despair,
He suddenly burst through a door and that Mayor
Discovered one shirker! Quite hidden away
In the Fairfax Apartments (Apartment 12-J)
A very small, *very* small shirker named Jo-Jo
Was standing, just standing, and bouncing a Yo-Yo!
Not making a sound! Not a yipp! Not a chirp!
And the Mayor rushed inside and he grabbed the young twerp!

And he climbed with the lad up the Eiffelberg Tower.

"This," cried the Mayor, "is your town's darkest hour!
The time for all *Whos* who have blood that is red
To come to the aid of their country!" he said.
"We've GOT to make noises in greater amounts!
So, open your mouth, lad! For every voice counts!"

Thus he spoke as he climbed. When they got to the top,
The lad cleared his throat and he shouted out, "YOPP!"

And the Yopp . . .
That one small, extra Yopp put it over!
Finally, at last! From that speck on that clover
Their voices were heard! They rang out clear and clean.
And the elephant smiled. "Do you see what I mean? . . .
They've proved they ARE persons, no matter how small.
And their whole world was saved by the Smallest of All!"

"How true! Yes, how true," said the big kangaroo.
"And, from now on, you know what I'm planning to do? . . .
From now on, I'm going to protect them with you!"
And the young kangaroo in her pouch said, . . .

"...ME, TOO!
From sun in the summer. From rain when it's fall-ish,
I'm going to protect them. No matter how small-ish!"

Speech bubbles: "IT IS, OLD MAN, IF YOU KNOW THE BIG GAME SPOTS!" / "SHUX! AND THEY TOLD ME THIS WAS A BIG GAME JUNGLE!"

These 1939 NBC ads were perhaps the inspiration for a similar scene in *Horton Hatches the Egg*.

THE ADMAN COMETH

In 1939, the year before Horton first appeared in Horton Hatches the Egg, *Ted Geisel put a Horton look-alike elephant to work selling radio ad spots for NBC. But Ted's career in advertising started years earlier, shortly after his "Medieval Tenant" cartoon (shown at right) appeared in* Judge *in 1927. An executive at Standard Oil liked the humorous way Ted had invoked the name of its popular insecticide, Flit, in the cartoon and offered Ted a contract to create ads for Flit, Essolube, Vico motor oil, and other products of Standard Oil. Many of the ads depicted gigantic, science fiction–type bugs and promised that Flit would kill them. It was this Seussian surreal sense of humor that proved that funny ads could sell products.*

MEDIÆVAL TENANT—*Darn it all, another Dragon. And just after I'd sprayed the whole castle with Flit!*

QUICK HENRY THE FLIT! IMPROVED WITH DDT

FLIT KILLS ROACHES, BEDBUGS, ANTS, FLIES and MOSQUITOES

Ted came up with the slogan "Quick, Henry, the Flit!" which became a household phrase in the 1930s and '40s.

Foil the Karbo-nockus!

Essolube 5-STAR MOTOR OIL Forms less carbon

All it needs is... Holly Sugar

ALL IT NEEDS IS... Holly Sugar

A series of ads for Holly Sugar appeared in the 1950s and were the last ads that Ted created.

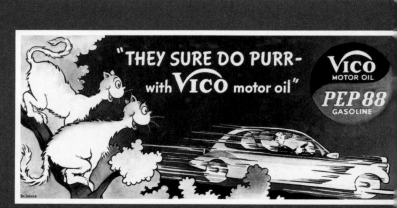

"THEY SURE DO PURR—with VICO motor oil" VICO MOTOR OIL PEP 88 GASOLINE

and enter the cat!

I do like green eggs and ham!

The first book that I ever read out loud was *Green Eggs and Ham*. I recited it to my entire family, which had assembled to hear five-year-old Christopher read; a harrowing experience that I never forgot.

But . . .

At that moment, I fell in love with one of the greatest children's authors, Theodor Seuss Geisel—otherwise known as Dr. Seuss. I read all of the Seuss books in my library and eventually found what became my favorite: *The Cat in the Hat*.

The Cat in the Hat is the story of two boring children who are left at home and do nothing but wait for their mother. Really! Then along comes the incorrigible Cat, and the mayhem commences as he proceeds to destroy nearly everything in the house. Of course he picks up the pieces in the end, but still, what child hasn't seen someone with perfectly combed hair and wanted to mess it up, or wanted to provoke someone with no sense of humor by rearranging their room while they were at the store? That's exactly what the Cat does. And when he leaves, you know that he could never resist upsetting the children's lives again, which he does in *The Cat in the Hat Comes Back*.

The Cat in the Hat was created when William Spaulding, the textbook publisher at Houghton Mifflin, commissioned Dr. Seuss to write a book that would encourage children to read. The one stipulation was that he could only use 225 words out of a list of 400 that they sent him.

Ouch! As an author myself, I cringe at the thought.

Stymied, Dr. Seuss finally decided that if he could find two words that rhymed, he would make them the book's title and subject. Those two were *cat* and *hat*. Once he had them, *The Cat in the Hat* still took nine months to finish. In total, Dr. Seuss used just 223 different words, a virtuoso writing performance akin to composing a symphony on a kazoo, using only one scale! Yet despite the limited vocabulary, Dr. Seuss created rhymes and rhythms that delight both children and adults.

Dr. Seuss was also an accomplished artist who illustrated his children's books. His work is now collected by people and museums around the world, and for good reason. With wild colors, loopy penmanship, and surreal images to match Dalí, Seuss invented a world that could be both safe and scary. His drawings of the Cat are perfect: jaunty, confident, and with a gleam of mischief in his eye. . . . Who could imagine Dr. Seuss without his art?

The Cat in the Hat is a story of danger and caution and of two children who finally gain the strength to say, "No!" I look forward to having my own kids read it one day. Master of the batty and loony, lord of the wacky and goony, all hail Dr. Seuss!

And enter the Cat!

CHRISTOPHER PAOLINI

a homeschooler who began writing the fantasy bestseller *Eragon* at age fifteen

the cat
in the hat

[ORIGINALLY PUBLISHED IN 1957]

The sun did not shine.
It was too wet to play.
So we sat in the house
All that cold, cold, wet day.

I sat there with Sally.
We sat there, we two.
And I said, "How I wish
We had something to do!"

Too wet to go out
And too cold to play ball.
So we sat in the house.
We did nothing at all.

So all we could do was to
Sit!
  Sit!
    Sit!
      Sit!
And we did not like it.
Not one little bit.

And then
Something went BUMP!
How that bump made us jump!

We looked!
Then we saw him step in on the mat!
We looked!
And we saw him!
The Cat in the Hat!
And he said to us,
"Why do you sit there like that?"

"I know it is wet
And the sun is not sunny.
But we can have
Lots of good fun that is funny!"

"I know some good games we could play,"
Said the cat.
"I know some new tricks,"
Said the Cat in the Hat.
"A lot of good tricks.
I will show them to you.
Your mother
Will not mind at all if I do."

Then Sally and I
Did not know what to say.
Our mother was out of the house
For the day.

124

But our fish said, "No! No!
Make that cat go away!
Tell that Cat in the Hat
You do NOT want to play.
He should not be here.
He should not be about.
He should not be here
When your mother is out!"

"Now! Now! Have no fear.
Have no fear!" said the cat.
"My tricks are not bad,"
Said the Cat in the Hat.
"Why, we can have
Lots of good fun, if you wish,
With a game that I call
UP-UP-UP with a fish!"

"Put me down!" said the fish.
"This is no fun at all!
Put me down!" said the fish.
"I do NOT wish to fall!"

"Have no fear!" said the cat.
"I will not let you fall.
I will hold you up high
As I stand on a ball.
With a book on one hand!
And a cup on my hat!
But that is not ALL I can do!"
Said the cat . . .

"Look at me!
Look at me now!" said the cat.
"With a cup and a cake
On the top of my hat!
I can hold up TWO books!
I can hold up the fish!
And a little toy ship!
And some milk on a dish!
And look!
I can hop up and down on the ball!
But that is not all!
Oh, no.
That is not all . . .

"Look at me!
Look at me!
Look at me NOW!
It is fun to have fun
But you have to know how.
I can hold up the cup
And the milk and the cake!
I can hold up these books!
And the fish on a rake!
I can hold the toy ship
And a little toy man!
And look! With my tail
I can hold a red fan!
I can fan with the fan
As I hop on the ball!
But that is not all.
Oh, no.
That is not all. . . ."

128

That is what the cat said . . .
Then he fell on his head!
He came down with a bump
From up there on the ball.
And Sally and I,
We saw ALL the things fall!

And our fish came down, too.
He fell into a pot!
He said, "Do I like this?
Oh, no! I do not.
This is not a good game,"
Said our fish as he lit.
"No, I do not like it,
Not one little bit!"

"Now look what you did!"
Said the fish to the cat.
"Now look at this house!
Look at this! Look at that!
You sank our toy ship,
Sank it deep in the cake.
You shook up our house
And you bent our new rake.
You SHOULD NOT be here
When our mother is not.
You get out of this house!"
Said the fish in the pot.

"But I like to be here.
Oh, I like it a lot!"
Said the Cat in the Hat
To the fish in the pot.
"I will NOT go away.
I do NOT wish to go!
And so," said the Cat in the Hat,
"So
     so
          so . . .
I will show you
Another good game that I know!"

And then he ran out.
And, then, fast as a fox,
The Cat in the Hat
Came back in with a box.

A big red wood box.
It was shut with a hook.
"Now look at this trick,"
Said the cat.
"Take a look!"

Then he got up on top
With a tip of his hat.
"I call this game FUN-IN-A-BOX,"
Said the cat.
"In this box are two things
I will show to you now.
You will like these two things,"
Said the cat with a bow.

"I will pick up the hook.
You will see something new.
Two things. And I call them
Thing One and Thing Two.
These Things will not bite you.
They want to have fun."
Then, out of the box
Came Thing Two and Thing One!
And they ran to us fast.
They said, "How do you do?
Would you like to shake hands
With Thing One and Thing Two?"

And Sally and I
Did not know what to do.
So we had to shake hands
With Thing One and Thing Two.
We shook their two hands.
But our fish said, "No! No!
Those Things should not be
In this house! Make them go!

"They should not be here
When your mother is not!
Put them out! Put them out!"
Said the fish in the pot.

"Have no fear, little fish,"
Said the Cat in the Hat.
"These Things are good Things."
And he gave them a pat.
"They are tame. Oh, so tame!
They have come here to play.
They will give you some fun
On this wet, wet, wet day."

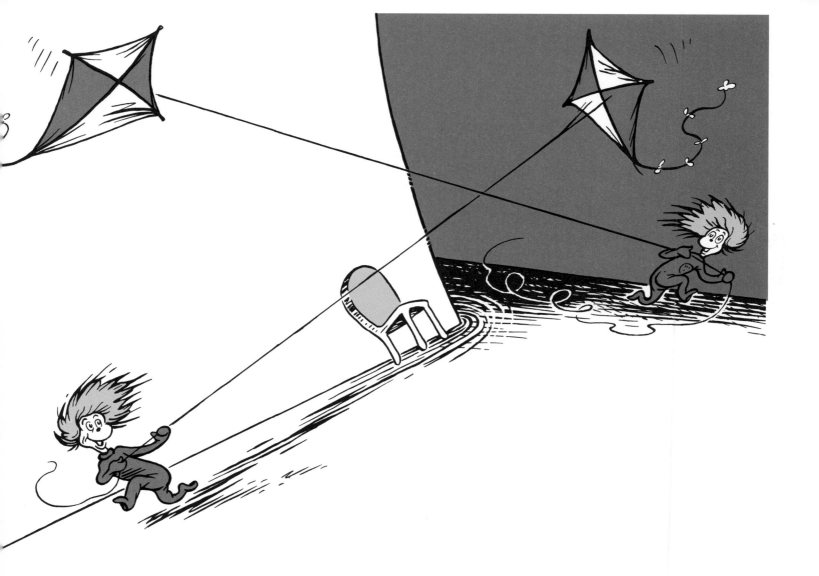

"Now, here is a game that they like,"
Said the cat.
"They like to fly kites,"
Said the Cat in the Hat.

"No! Not in the house!"
Said the fish in the pot.
"They should not fly kites
In a house! They should not.
Oh, the things they will bump!
Oh, the things they will hit!
Oh, I do not like it!
Not one little bit!"

Then Sally and I
Saw them run down the hall.
We saw those two Things
Bump their kites on the wall!
Bump! Thump! Thump! Bump!
Down the wall in the hall.

Thing Two and Thing One!
They ran up! They ran down!
On the string of one kite
We saw Mother's new gown!
Her gown with the dots
That are pink, white and red.
Then we saw one kite bump
On the head of her bed!

Then those Things ran about
With big bumps, jumps and kicks
And with hops and big thumps
And all kinds of bad tricks.
And I said,
"I do NOT like the way that they play!
If Mother could see this,
Oh, what would she say!"

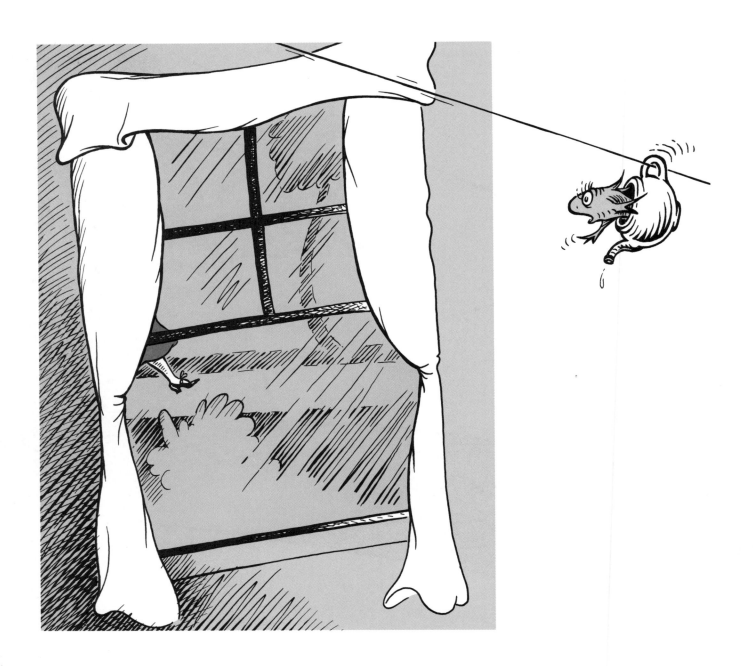

Then our fish said, "LOOK! LOOK!"
And our fish shook with fear.
"Your mother is on her way home!
Do you hear?
Oh, what will she do to us?
What will she say?
Oh, she will not like it
To find us this way!"

"So, DO something! Fast!" said the fish.
"Do you hear!
I saw her. Your mother!
Your mother is near!
So, as fast as you can,
Think of something to do!
You will have to get rid of
Thing One and Thing Two!"

So, as fast as I could,
I went after my net.
And I said, "With my net
I can get them I bet.
I bet, with my net,
I can get those Things yet!"

Then I let down my net.
It came down with a PLOP!
And I had them! At last!
Those two Things had to stop.
Then I said to the cat,
"Now you do as I say.
You pack up those Things
And you take them away!"

"Oh dear!" said the cat.
"You did not like our game . . .
Oh dear.
What a shame!
What a shame!
What a shame!"

149

Then he shut up the Things
In the box with the hook.
And the cat went away
With a sad kind of look.

"That is good," said the fish.
"He has gone away. Yes.
But your mother will come.
She will find this big mess!
And this mess is so big
And so deep and so tall,
We can not pick it up.
There is no way at all!"

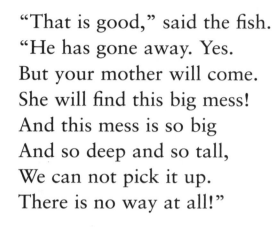

And THEN!
Who was back in the house?
Why, the cat!
"Have no fear of this mess,"
Said the Cat in the Hat.
"I always pick up all my playthings
And so . . .
I will show you another
Good trick that I know!"

Then we saw him pick up
All the things that were down.
He picked up the cake,
And the rake, and the gown,
And the milk, and the strings,
And the books, and the dish,
And the fan, and the cup,
And the ship, and the fish.
And he put them away.
Then he said, "That is that."
And then he was gone
With a tip of his hat.

Then our mother came in
And she said to us two,
"Did you have any fun?
Tell me. What did you do?"

And Sally and I did not know
What to say.
Should we tell her
The things that went on there that day?

Should we tell her about it?
Now, what SHOULD we do?
Well . . .
What would YOU do
If your mother asked YOU?

"A Plethora of Cats," oil on canvas, 1970.

"Joseph Katz and His Coat of Many Colors," acrylic on canvas board, 1970.

Preliminary sketches (above and far right) for *The Cat in the Hat Songbook*, published 1967.

COOL CAT AFTER HOURS

Ted always drew cats, but after he published The Cat in the Hat, *sly felines took on a more dominant role, especially in the paintings he created for his own pleasure late at night when he took a break from working on a book. "A Plethora of Cats" was one of his favorite paintings and still hangs in his home in La Jolla.*

Beginner Books

Box 1924, La Jolla, California

T. S. Geisel, PRESIDENT

Poodle with his left hand. Camel with his right hand.

...with his left big toe.

the true spirit of the grinch

The Grinch has become as closely associated with Christmas as Santa Claus, Scrooge, and Rudolph. But like the Christmases he detested, the Grinch has gotten more elaborate over the years. When Ted Geisel's book first appeared in October 1957, the Grinch wasn't even green—that change took place in Chuck Jones's famous 1966 interpretation, voiced by Boris Karloff. The succeeding decades had Emmy-winning iterations under directors Gerard Baldwin in *Halloween Is Grinch Night* (1977) and Bill Perez in *The Grinch Grinches the Cat in the Hat* (1982). For the new century, a backstory with movie tie-ins created "da Grinch" to accompany Ron Howard's vision, as seen through Jim Carrey's makeup and mayhem. For all their wonders, they lack the simplicity of Ted's black-outlined, pink-eyed original.

Although readers associate Dr. Seuss most closely with the puckish Cat in the Hat, Ted identified equally with the Grinch, opting for a California "GRINCH" license plate for many years. Ted's concern about the commercialization of the holiday season dates back at least to his college days. The December 15, 1924, issue of Dartmouth's *Jack-O-Lantern* contained Ted's "Santy Claus Be Hanged." In it, he suggested a gift exchange to rectify all the disappointing, inappropriate gifts that people get, as when "Sister wanted silk unmentionables and she gets burlap unpronounceables." Those feelings continued, and in the December 1957 issue of *Redbook*, Ted related that on the day after Christmas the previous year, he saw "a very Grinch-ish countenance in the mirror" and realized that "something had gone wrong with Christmas . . . or more likely with me. So I wrote the story . . . to see if I could rediscover something about Christmas that obviously I'd lost." It is no coincidence that Ted was fifty-three years old when he penned the Grinch's complaint, "For fifty-three years I've put up with it now! I MUST stop this Christmas from coming! . . . *But HOW?*"

But perhaps too much attention has been lavished on the anti-consumerist message in Ted's story. It isn't just the din of countless toys that bothers the Grinch. The thing that he specifically likes least of all is the Who-Christmas-Sing. He hates the sense of community among the Whos— the way that they "Would stand close together, with Christmas bells ringing. They'd stand hand-in-hand. And the *Whos* would start singing!" More than a treatise against rampant consumerism, the book promotes inclusiveness—a common theme in Ted's stories, which often taught children tolerance. The real message of the book involves the true spirit of community, which has been lost. In typical Ted fashion, although this is a Christmas tale, religion does not enter into the story, for that might prove unintentionally divisive or exclusionary. Even on the rare occasion when he addressed God, as he did two years earlier in the December 23, 1955, issue of *Collier's* in "A Prayer for a Child," Ted's message promoted the same communal spirit that the Grinch would soon learn:

> *Please tell all men*
> *That Peace is Good.*
> *That's all*
> *That need be understood.*

CHARLES D. COHEN

world's foremost collector of Seussiana and author of
The Seuss, the Whole Seuss, and Nothing but the Seuss

how the grinch stole christmas!

[ORIGINALLY PUBLISHED IN 1957]

Every *Who*
Down in *Who*-ville
Liked Christmas a lot . . .

But the Grinch,
Who lived just north of *Who*-ville,
Did NOT!

The Grinch *hated* Christmas! The whole Christmas season!
Now, please don't ask why. No one quite knows the reason.
It *could* be his head wasn't screwed on just right.
It *could* be, perhaps, that his shoes were too tight.
But I think that the most likely reason of all
May have been that his heart was two sizes too small.

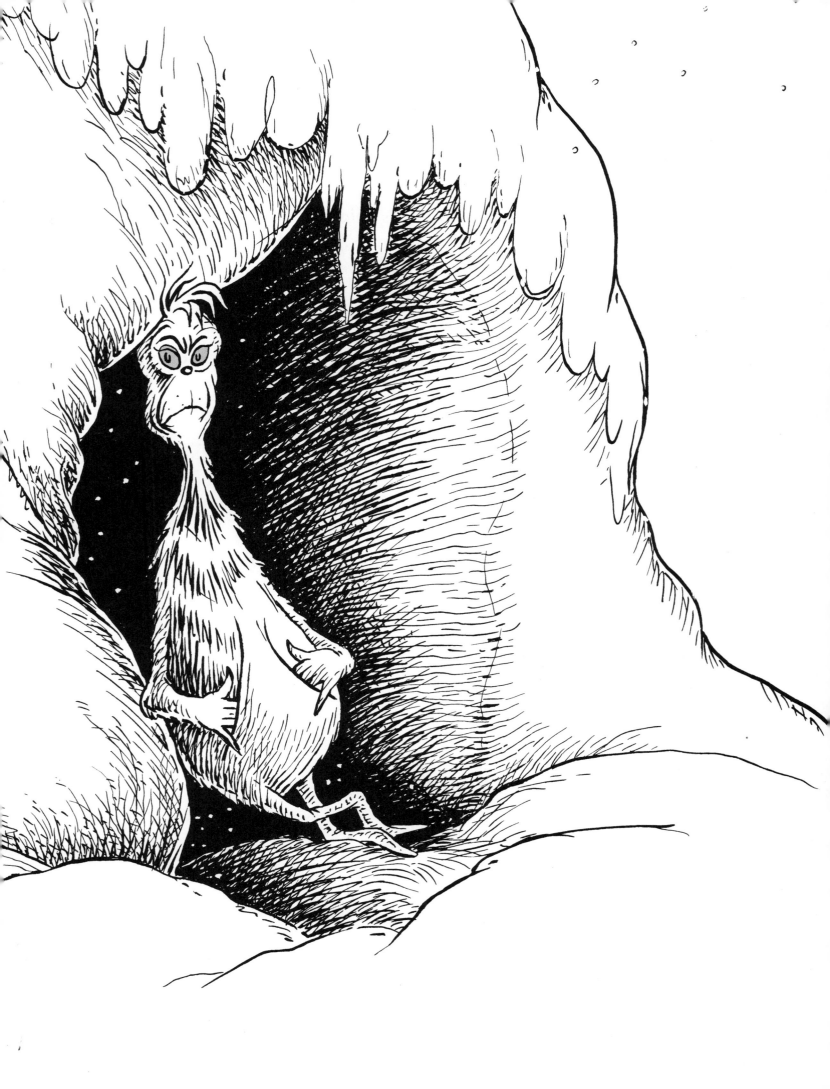

But,
Whatever the reason,
His heart or his shoes,
He stood there on Christmas Eve, hating the *Whos*,
Staring down from his cave with a sour, Grinchy frown
At the warm lighted windows below in their town.
For he knew every *Who* down in *Who*-ville beneath
Was busy now, hanging a mistletoe wreath.

"And they're hanging their stockings!" he snarled with a sneer.
"Tomorrow is Christmas! It's practically here!"
Then he growled, with his Grinch fingers nervously drumming,
"I MUST find some way to stop Christmas from coming!"

For,
Tomorrow, he knew...

. . . All the *Who* girls and boys
Would wake bright and early. They'd rush for their toys!
And *then!* Oh, the noise! Oh, the Noise! Noise! Noise! Noise!
That's *one* thing he hated! The NOISE! NOISE! NOISE! NOISE!

Then the *Whos*, young and old, would sit down to a feast.
And they'd feast! *And they'd feast!*
And they'd FEAST!
   FEAST!
    FEAST!
     FEAST!
They would feast on *Who*-pudding, and rare *Who*-roast-beast
Which was something the Grinch couldn't stand in the least!

And THEN
They'd do something
He liked least of all!
Every *Who* down in *Who*-ville, the tall and the small,
Would stand close together, with Christmas bells ringing.
They'd stand hand-in-hand. And the *Whos* would start singing!

They'd sing! *And they'd sing!*
AND they'd SING! SING! SING! SING!
And the more the Grinch thought of this *Who*-Christmas-Sing,
The more the Grinch thought, "I must stop this whole thing!
"Why, for fifty-three years I've put up with it now!
"I MUST stop this Christmas from coming!
                                      ...But HOW?"

Then he got an idea!
An awful idea!
THE GRINCH
GOT A WONDERFUL, AWFUL IDEA!

"I know *just* what to do!" The Grinch laughed in his throat.
And he made a quick Santy Claus hat and a coat.
And he chuckled, and clucked, "What a great Grinchy trick!
"With this coat and this hat, I look just like Saint Nick!"

"All I need is a reindeer . . ."
The Grinch looked around.
But, since reindeer are scarce, there was none to be found.
Did that stop the old Grinch . . . ?
No! The Grinch simply said,
"If I can't *find* a reindeer, I'll *make* one instead!"
So he called his dog, Max. Then he took some red thread
And he tied a big horn on the top of his head.

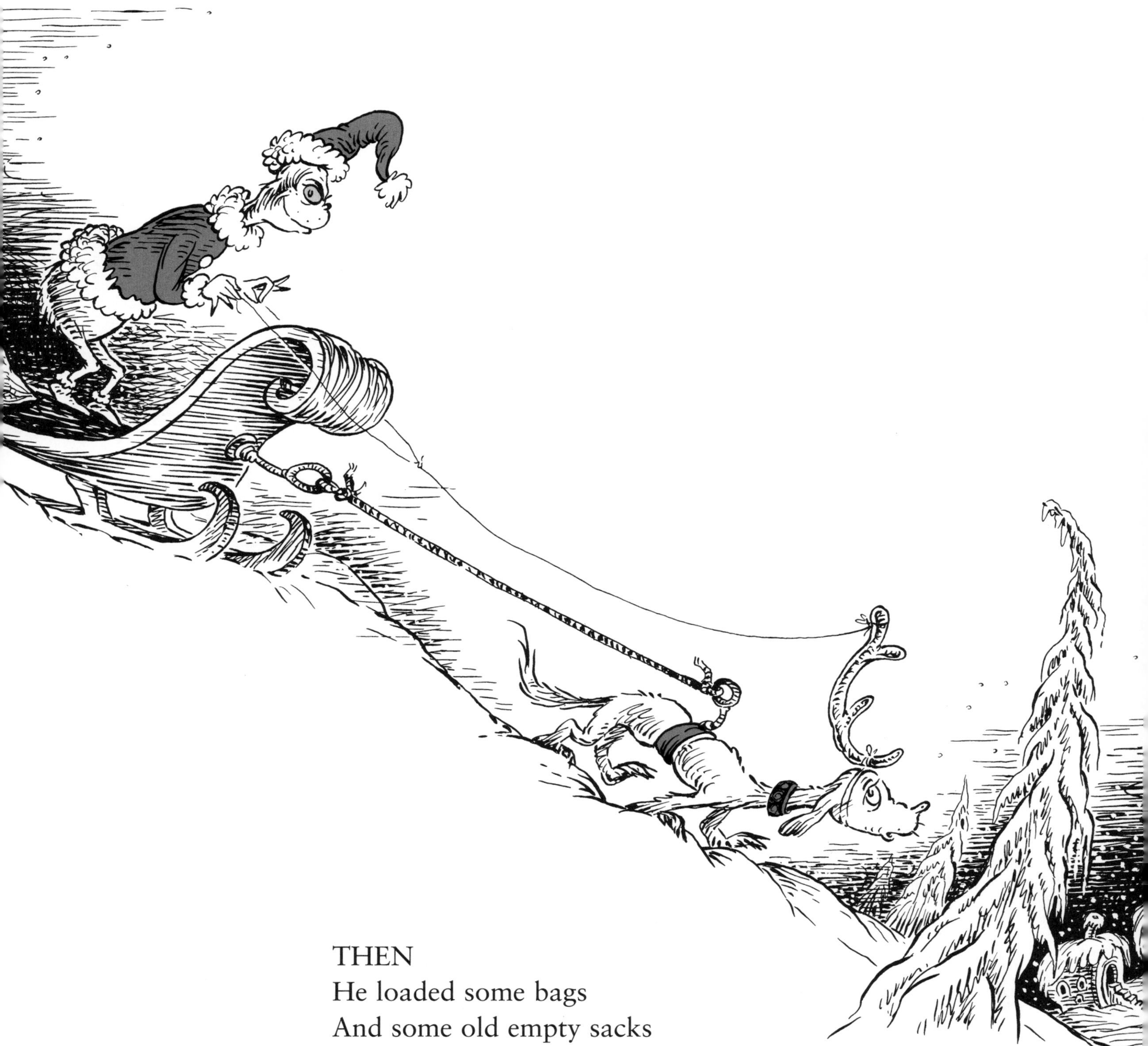

THEN
He loaded some bags
And some old empty sacks
On a ramshackle sleigh
And he hitched up old Max.

Then the Grinch said, "Giddap!"
And the sleigh started down
Toward the homes where the *Whos*
Lay a-snooze in their town.

All their windows were dark. Quiet snow filled the air.
All the *Whos* were all dreaming sweet dreams without care
When he came to the first little house on the square.
"This is stop number one," the old Grinchy Claus hissed
And he climbed to the roof, empty bags in his fist.

Then he slid down the chimney. A rather tight pinch.
But, if Santa could do it, then so could the Grinch.
He got stuck only once, for a moment or two.
Then he stuck his head out of the fireplace flue
Where the little *Who* stockings all hung in a row.
"These stockings," he grinned, "are the *first* things to go!"

171

Then he slithered and slunk, with a smile most unpleasant,
Around the whole room, and he took every present!
Pop guns! And bicycles! Roller skates! Drums!
Checkerboards! Tricycles! Popcorn! And plums!
And he stuffed them in bags. Then the Grinch, very nimbly,
Stuffed all the bags, one by one, up the chimbley!

Then he slunk to the icebox.
He took the *Whos'* feast!
He took the *Who*-pudding!
He took the roast beast!
He cleaned out that icebox
   as quick as a flash.
Why, that Grinch even took
   their last can of *Who*-hash!

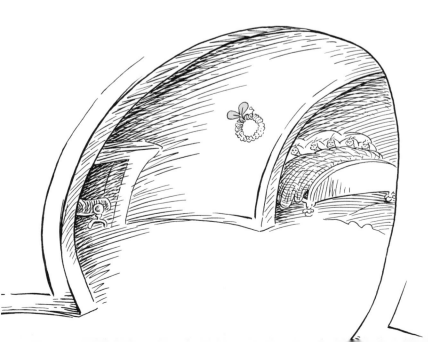

Then he stuffed all the food
   up the chimney with glee.
"And NOW!" grinned the Grinch,
"I will stuff up the tree!"

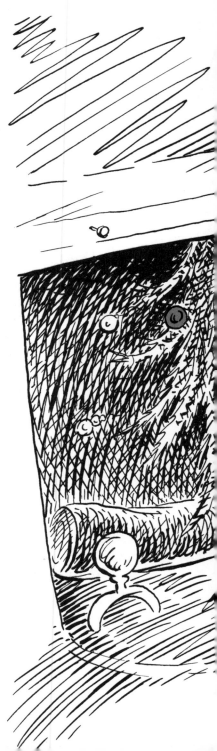

And the Grinch grabbed the tree, and he started to shove
When he heard a small sound like the coo of a dove.
He turned around fast, and he saw a small *Who!*
Little Cindy-Lou *Who,* who was not more than two.

The Grinch had been caught by this tiny *Who* daughter
Who'd got out of bed for a cup of cold water.
She stared at the Grinch and said, "Santy Claus, why,
"*Why* are you taking our Christmas tree? WHY?"

But, you know, that old Grinch was so smart and so slick
He thought up a lie, and he thought it up quick!
"Why, my sweet little tot," the fake Santy Claus lied,
"There's a light on this tree that won't light on one side.
"So I'm taking it home to my workshop, my dear.
"I'll fix it up *there*. Then I'll bring it back *here*."

And his fib fooled the child. Then he patted her head
And he got her a drink and he sent her to bed.
And when Cindy-Lou *Who* went to bed with her cup,
HE went to the chimney and stuffed the tree up!

Then the *last* thing he took
Was the log for their fire!
Then he went up the chimney, himself, the old liar.
On their walls he left nothing but hooks and some wire.

And the one speck of food
That he left in the house
Was a crumb that was even too small for a mouse.

THEN
He did the *same* thing
To the *other Whos'* houses

Leaving crumbs
Much too small
For the other *Whos'* mouses!

179

MERRY MERRY

It was quarter past dawn . . .
    All the *Whos,* still a-bed,
    All the *Whos,* still a-snooze
When he packed up his sled,
Packed it up with their presents! The ribbons! The wrappings!
The tags! And the tinsel! The trimmings! The trappings!

Three thousand feet up! Up the side of Mt. Crumpit,
He rode with his load to the tiptop to dump it!
"Pooh-Pooh to the *Whos!*" he was grinch-ish-ly humming.
"They're finding out now that no Christmas is coming!
"They're just waking up! I know *just* what they'll do!
"Their mouths will hang open a minute or two
"Then the *Whos* down in *Who*-ville will all cry BOO-HOO!

"That's a noise," grinned the Grinch,
"That I simply MUST hear!"
So he paused. And the Grinch put his hand to his ear.
And he *did* hear a sound rising over the snow.
It started in low. Then it started to grow . . .

But the sound wasn't *sad*!
Why, this sound sounded *merry*!
It *couldn't* be so!
But it WAS merry! VERY!

He stared down at *Who*-ville!
The Grinch popped his eyes!
Then he shook!
What he saw was a shocking surprise!

Every *Who* down in *Who*-ville, the tall and the small,
Was singing! Without any presents at all!

He HADN'T stopped Christmas from coming!
IT CAME!
Somehow or other, it came just the same!

And the Grinch, with his grinch-feet ice-cold in the snow,
Stood puzzling and puzzling: "How *could* it be so?
"It came without ribbons! It came without tags!
"It came without packages, boxes or bags!"
And he puzzled three hours, till his puzzler was sore.
Then the Grinch thought of something he hadn't before!
"Maybe Christmas," he thought, "*doesn't* come from a store.
"Maybe Christmas . . . perhaps . . . means a little bit more!"

And what happened *then* . . . ?
Well . . . in *Who*-ville they say
That the Grinch's small heart
Grew three sizes that day!
And the minute his heart didn't feel quite so tight,
He whizzed with his load through the bright morning light
And he brought back the toys! And the food for the feast!
And he . . .

...HE HIMSELF...!
The Grinch carved the roast beast!

The Hoobub and the Grinch

BY DR. SEUSS

The Hoobub was lying outdoors in the sun,
The wonderful, wonderful, warm summer sun.
"There's *nothing*," he said, "quite as good as the sun!"

Then, up walked a Grinch with a piece of green string.
"How much," asked the Grinch, "will you pay for this thing?
You sure ought to have it. You'll find it great fun.
And it's worth a lot more than that old-fashioned sun."
"Huh . . . ?" asked the Hoobub. "Sounds silly to me.
Worth more than the sun . . . ? Why, that surely can't be."
"But it *is!*" grinned the Grinch. "Let me give you the reasons.

The sun's only good in a couple short seasons.
For you'll have to admit that in winter and fall
The sun is quite weak. It is not strong at all.
*But this wonderful piece of green string I have here
Is strong, my good friend, every month of the year!*"
"Even so . . ." said the Hoobub, "I still sort of doubt . . ."
"But you *know*," yapped the Grinch, and he started to shout,
"That *sometimes* the sun doesn't even come out!
But this marvelous piece of green string, I declare,
*Can come out of your pocket, if you keep it there,
Any time, day or night! Any place! Anywhere!*"

"Hmm . . ." said the Hoobub. "That *would* be quite handy . . ."
"This piece of green string," yelled the Grinch, "is a dandy!
That sun, let me tell you, is dangerous stuff!
It can freckle your face. It can make your skin rough.
When the sun gets too hot, it can broil you like fat!
But this piece of green string, sir, will NEVER do that!
THIS PIECE OF GREEN STRING IS COLOSSAL! IMMENSE!
AND, TO YOU . . . WELL, I'LL SELL IT FOR 98 CENTS!"
And the Hoobub . . . *he bought!*
(And I'm sorry to say
That Grinches sell Hoobubs such things every day.)

This story appeared in *Redbook* in May 1955,
two years before *How the Grinch Stole
Christmas!* was published. In it, a Grinch
is a con artist with little resemblance to
the Grinch.

Seuss looking like a Grinch

Self-portrait,
December 26, 1956.

Ted's California license plate.

THE DARKER SIDE OF SEUSS

*It is believed that Ted Geisel
identified with the Cat in the
Hat, that sly instigator of
unruly fun. But a part of him
also bonded with that sourpuss
killjoy, the Grinch. Though Ted
was incapable of being nasty,
he has confessed to some very
Grinchy thoughts!*

Ted (left) with animator
Chuck Jones on the MGM-TV
set of *How the Grinch Stole
Christmas!*, 1966.

yertle, hitler, and dr. seuss

And the turtles, of course...
all the turtles are free
As turtles and, maybe,
all creatures should be.

These famous final lines from *Yertle the Turtle* tip us off to the fact that Dr. Seuss is teaching us a lesson. In fact, it is a rare Dr. Seuss book that does *not* teach, although his artistry—here, the "and, maybe, all creatures"—is such that the teaching often sneaks in under our anti-teaching radar. In *The Lorax* (Dr. Seuss's favorite among his own books) and *The Butter Battle Book,* the teaching is more obvious. In others, it is less obvious—*The Cat in the Hat,* for example. But even that book has its message. Said Dr. Seuss in 1983: "*The Cat in the Hat* is a revolt against authority, but it's ameliorated by the fact that the Cat cleans up everything at the end."

Yertle the Turtle falls somewhere in the middle; the message is not obvious, but it's not hidden, either. John Q. Public (personified by a turtle named Mack) faces off against a power-hungry leader (King Yertle), and, ultimately, Mack's great burp brings Yertle down. (In 1958, Dr. Seuss's editors didn't object to the teaching, but they worried that the word *burp* was off-color!)

Few readers—young or old—realize that Yertle is Adolf Hitler. In his editorial cartoons of 1941–42 in the New York newspaper *PM,* Dr. Seuss had used turtles—most notably in the "V for Victory" cartoon of March 1942, shown on page 207, which also prefigures the tower of turtles in *Yertle the Turtle.* But the turtles of 1942 were "dawdling producers," not Hitler. In the cartoons of 1941–42, Dr. Seuss drew a recognizable

Hitler, also shown on page 207.

But Yertle *is* Hitler. Here's what Dr. Seuss said in a 1987 interview: "Yertle was Hitler or Mussolini. Originally, Yertle had a mustache, but I took it off. I thought it was gilding the lily a bit." To be sure, the parallel breaks down, for what ended Hitler's career was no burp from below; it was the Allied Forces attacking from outside. Still, Dr. Seuss said in 1983, "There's *Yertle the Turtle,* which was modeled on the rise of Hitler; and then there's *The Sneetches,* which was inspired by my opposition to anti-Semitism. These books come from . . . the part of my soul that started out to be a teacher."

Dr. Seuss a teacher? Of course! A teacher of tolerance (*The Sneetches*). A teacher of reading (all the Beginner Books, starting with *The Cat in the Hat*). A teacher of ecological awareness (*The Lorax*). A teacher against the nuclear arms race (*The Butter Battle Book*). A teacher of sympathy for the underdog (*Yertle the Turtle*).

"I'm naïve enough to believe," Dr. Seuss said in 1984, "that society will be changed by examination of ideas through books and the press, and that information can prove to be greater than the dissemination of stupidity." Even on his deathbed in 1991, Dr. Seuss was still teaching: "The best slogan I can think of to leave with the kids of the U.S.A. would be: 'We can . . . and we've got to . . . do better than this.'" Then he crossed out *the kids of,* so the message became more general, for all of us, his readers of all ages. As Dr. Seuss himself had put it much earlier, "Outside of my Beginner Books, I never write for children. I write for people."

RICHARD H. MINEAR

professor of history at the University of Massachusetts at Amherst and author of *Dr. Seuss Goes to War*

yertle the turtle

[ORIGINALLY PUBLISHED IN 1958]

On the far-away Island of Sala-ma-Sond,
Yertle the Turtle was king of the pond.
A nice little pond. It was clean. It was neat.
The water was warm. There was plenty to eat.
The turtles had everything turtles might need.
And they were all happy. Quite happy indeed.

They *were* . . . until Yertle, the king of them all,
Decided the kingdom he ruled was too small.
"I'm ruler," said Yertle, "of all that I see.
But I don't see *enough*. That's the trouble with me.
With this stone for a throne, I look down on my pond
But I cannot look down on the places beyond.
This throne that I sit on is too, too low down.
It ought to be *higher*!" he said with a frown.
"If I could sit high, how much greater I'd be!
What a king! I'd be ruler of all I could see!"

So Yertle, the Turtle King, lifted his hand
And Yertle, the Turtle King, gave a command.
He ordered nine turtles to swim to his stone
And, using these turtles, he built a *new* throne.
He made each turtle stand on another one's back
And he piled them all up in a nine-turtle stack.
And then Yertle climbed up. He sat down on the pile.
What a wonderful view! He could see 'most a mile!

"All mine!" Yertle cried. "Oh, the things I now rule!
I'm king of a cow! And I'm king of a mule!
I'm king of a house! And, what's more, beyond that,
I'm king of a blueberry bush and a cat!
I'm Yertle the Turtle! Oh, marvelous me!
For I am the ruler of all that I see!"

And all through that morning, he sat there up high
Saying over and over, "A great king am I!"
Until 'long about noon. Then he heard a faint sigh.
"What's *that*?" snapped the king
And he looked down the stack.
And he saw, at the bottom, a turtle named Mack.
Just a part of his throne. And this plain little turtle
Looked up and he said, "Beg your pardon, King Yertle.
I've pains in my back and my shoulders and knees.
How long must we stand here, Your Majesty, please?"

"SILENCE!" the King of the Turtles barked back.
"I'm king, and you're only a turtle named Mack."

"You stay in your place while I sit here and rule.
I'm king of a cow! And I'm king of a mule!
I'm king of a house! And a bush! And a cat!
But that isn't all. I'll do better than *that*!
My throne shall be *higher*!" his royal voice thundered,
"So pile up more turtles! I want 'bout two hundred!"

"Turtles! More turtles!" he bellowed and brayed.
And the turtles 'way down in the pond were afraid.
They trembled. They shook. But they came. They obeyed.
From all over the pond, they came swimming by dozens.
Whole families of turtles, with uncles and cousins.
And all of them stepped on the head of poor Mack.
One after another, they climbed up the stack.

THEN Yertle the Turtle was perched up so high,
He could see forty miles from his throne in the sky!
"Hooray!" shouted Yertle. "I'm king of the trees!
I'm king of the birds! And I'm king of the bees!
I'm king of the butterflies! King of the air!
Ah, me! What a throne! What a wonderful chair!
I'm Yertle the Turtle! Oh, marvelous me!
For I am the ruler of all that I see!"

Then again, from below, in the great heavy stack,
Came a groan from that plain little turtle named Mack.
"Your Majesty, please . . . I don't like to complain,
But down here below, we are feeling great pain.
I know, up on top you are seeing great sights,
But down at the bottom we, too, should have rights.
We turtles can't stand it. Our shells will all crack!
Besides, we need food. We are starving!" groaned Mack.

"You hush up your mouth!" howled the mighty King Yertle.
"You've no right to talk to the world's highest turtle.
I rule from the clouds! Over land! Over sea!
There's nothing, no, NOTHING, that's higher than me!"

But, while he was shouting, he saw with surprise
That the moon of the evening was starting to rise
Up over his head in the darkening skies.
"What's THAT?" snorted Yertle. "Say, what IS that thing
That dares to be higher than Yertle the King?
I shall not allow it! I'll go higher still!
I'll build my throne higher! I can and I will!
I'll call some more turtles. I'll stack 'em to heaven!
I need 'bout five thousand, six hundred and seven!"

But, as Yertle, the Turtle King, lifted his hand
And started to order and give the command,
That plain little turtle below in the stack,
That plain little turtle whose name was just Mack,
Decided he'd taken enough. And he had.
And that plain little lad got a little bit mad
And that plain little Mack did a plain little thing.
He burped!
And his burp shook the throne of the king!

And Yertle the Turtle, the king of the trees,
The king of the air and the birds and the bees,
The king of a house and a cow and a mule . . .
Well, *that* was the end of the Turtle King's rule!
For Yertle, the King of all Sala-ma-Sond,
Fell off his high throne and fell *Plunk*! in the pond!

And today the great Yertle, that Marvelous he,
Is King of the Mud. That is all he can see.
And the turtles, of course . . . all the turtles are free
As turtles and, maybe, all creatures should be.

You Can't Build
A Substantial
V
Out of
Turtles!

DAWDLING PRODUCERS

March 20, 1942.

WORLD WAR II CARTOONS

Ted Geisel's political cartoons for the liberal New York newspaper PM *began appearing early in 1941. His motivation was to attack American isolationists. After December 7, 1941, when the U.S. entered the war, his cartoons often focused on the home front. The cartoon about "dawdling producers," represented as turtles (left), was aimed at slackers and labor disputes that were slowing the production of defense material. The V in that cartoon was wartime shorthand for "Victory."*

Our Big Bertha

February 18, 1942.

The head eats . . .
. . . the rest gets milked

CONSOLIDATED WORLD DAIRY
A. HITLER, Prop.

JUGO SLAVIA   ROMANIA   GREECE   AUSTRIA
BELGIUM
HOLLAND
DENMARK
NORWAY
POLAND
CZECHO SLOVAKIA   FRANCE

May 19, 1941.

Sure an' one day while you celebrate
The 'wearin' o' the Green,
I'll bring back snakes to Ireland
On a Nazi submarine.

IRELAND

March 17, 1942.

The Seussian menagerie and wit also savaged discrimination and anti-Semitism as un-American. Not surprisingly, another favorite target was Hitler. In January 1943, Ted traded in his pen and ink for a U.S. Army uniform and the brilliant cartoons ceased.

no holiday is more important

Thirty years ago I went to Australia to teach and was assigned to a class of thirty-eight four-and-a-half-year-old children in a remote rural town. Never having taught kindergarten and lacking virtually all school resources, I wondered how I could come up with something that not only would interest the children but would fulfill the school's list of prescribed literacy expectations.

Then I remembered Dr. Seuss. I bought a few of his books—*Green Eggs and Ham, The Cat in the Hat, One Fish Two Fish Red Fish Blue Fish*—Dr. Seuss being one of the few American children's book authors whose books were readily available in Australia, and began developing early reading lessons around them. The children responded far beyond my expectations. To my great relief, they were having fun learning to "read" by memorizing and were getting ready to take the next step toward becoming real readers.

Since then I've taught kindergarten in the New York City public schools for over twenty years and have seen many changes in early-childhood education, particularly in literacy instruction. But one constant has been the use of books by Dr. Seuss.

In addition to the easy-to-read ones written specifically to help children learn to read, such as those books mentioned above, I like to use *Happy Birthday to You!* in my classroom every year. No holiday is more important to young children than their birthday. *Happy Birthday to You!* generates discussions around the central question in the book: If you could have a "day of all days," what would it be like? Kindergartners need no encouragement to stretch their imaginations! I think Dr. Seuss would be the first to acknowledge that some of their wish lists rival his for sheer imaginative fun.

William would play chess against everybody—and win every time.

Maha would go to Hollywood and turn herself into a book that reads and shows pictures.

Charlotte expressed her birthday wish in a free-spirited dance interpretation of a princess being locked in a tower, awaiting her prince (possibly the little boy in her class whose affections she shared).

And Bryn would "ride in a horse-drawn wagon and see stuff I never saw before."

At the end of the book, Dr. Seuss tells children to shout loud and remember, "I am what I am! That's a great thing to be! If I say so myself, HAPPY BIRTHDAY TO ME!" Knowing yourself, trusting yourself, is a theme in many Dr. Seuss books and is just one of the many reasons why his stories stay with us long after we are children.

BARBARA MASON

kindergarten teacher in the New York City public schools

happy
birthday
to you!

[ORIGINALLY PUBLISHED IN 1959]

I wish we could do what they do in Katroo.
They sure know how to say "Happy Birthday to You!"

In Katroo, every year, on the day you were born
They start the day right in the bright early morn
When the Birthday Honk-Honker hikes high up Mt. Zorn
And lets loose a big blast on the big Birthday Horn.
And the voice of the horn calls out loud as it plays:
"Wake Up! For today is your Day of all Days!"

Then, the moment the Horn's happy honk-honk is heard,
Comes a fluttering flap-flap! And then comes THE BIRD!

The Great Birthday Bird!
And, so far as I know,
Katroo is the only place Birthday Birds grow.
This bird has a brain. He's most beautifully brained
With the brainiest bird-brain that's ever been trained.
He was trained by the most splendid Club in this nation,
The Katroo Happy Birthday Asso-see-eye-ation.
And, whether your name is Pete, Polly or Paul,
When your birthday comes round, he's in charge of it all.

Whether your name is Nate, Nelly or Ned,
He knows your address, and he heads for your be
You hear a soft *swoosh* in the brightening sky.
You are not all awake. But you open one eye.
Then over the housetops and trees of Katroo,
You see that bird coming! To you. *Just to you!*

That Bird pops right in!
You are up on your feet!
You jump to the window! You meet and you greet
With the Secret Katroo Birthday Hi-Sign-and-Shake
That only good people with birthdays may make.
You do it just so. With each finger and toe.
Then the Bird says, "Come on! Brush your teeth and let's go!
It's your Day of all Days! It's the Best of the Best!
So don't waste a minute!
Hop to it!
Get dressed!"

And five minutes later, you're having a snack
On your way out of town on a Smorgasbord's back.
"Today," laughs the Bird, "eat whatever you want.
Today no one tells you you cawnt or you shawnt.
And, today, you don't have to be tidy or neat.
If you wish, you may eat with both hands and both feet.
So get in there and munch. Have a big munch-er-oo!
Today is your birthday! *Today you are you!*"

If we didn't have birthdays, you wouldn't be you.
If you'd never been born, well then what would you do?
If you'd never been born, well then what would you be?
You *might* be a fish! Or a toad in a tree!
You might be a doorknob! Or three baked potatoes!
You might be a bag full of hard green tomatoes.
Or worse than all that . . . Why, you might be a WASN'T!
A Wasn't has no fun at all. No, he doesn't.
A Wasn't just isn't. He just isn't present.
But you . . . You ARE YOU! And, now isn't that pleasant!

So we'll go to the top of the toppest blue space,
The Official Katroo Birthday Sounding-Off Place!
Come on! Open your mouth and sound off at the sky!
Shout loud at the top of your voice, "I AM I!
ME!
I am I!
And I may not know why
But I know that I like it.
Three cheers! I AM I!"

And now, on this Day of all Days in Katroo,
The Asso-see-eye-ation has built just for you
A railway with very particular boats
That are pulled through the air by Funicular Goats.
These goats never slip, never trip, never bungle.
They'll take us down fast to the Birthday Flower Jungle.
The best-sniffing flowers that anyone grows
We have grown to be sniffed by your own private nose.

They smell like licorice! And cheese!
Send forty Who-Bubs up the trees
To snip with snippers! Nip with nippers!
Clip and clop with clapping clippers.
Nip and snip with clipping cloppers!
Snip and snop with snipping snoppers!
All for you, the Who-Bubs clip!
Happy Birthday! Nop and nip!

Then pile the wondrous-smelling stacks
On fifty Hippo-Heimers' backs!
They'll take those flowers all home for you.
You can keep the Hippo-Heimers too.

While this is done, I've got a hunch
It's time to eat our Birthday Lunch . . .

For Birthday luncheons, as a rule,
We serve hot dogs, rolled on a spool.

So stuff and stuff
And stuff and stuff
And stuff until you've had enough.

219

Now, of course, we're all mustard,
So, one of the rules
Is to wash it all off in the Mustard-Off Pools
Which are very fine warm-water mountaintop tubs
Which were built, just for this, by the Mustard-Off Clubs.

Then, out of the water! Sing loud while you dry!
Sing loud, "I am lucky!" Sing loud, "I am I!"

If you'd never been born, then you might be an ISN'T!
An Isn't has no fun at all. No he disn't.
He never has birthdays, and that isn't pleasant.
You have to be born, or you don't get a present.

A Present! *A-ha!*
Now what kind shall I give . . . ?
Why, the kind you'll remember
As long as you live!

Would you like a fine pet?
Well, that's just what you'll get.
I'll get you the fanciest pet ever yet!

As you see, we have here in the heart of our nation
The Official Katroo Birthday Pet Reservation.
From east of the East-est to west of the West-est
We've searched the whole world just to bring you the best-est.
They come in all sizes . . . small, medium, tall.
If you wish, I will find you the tallest of all!

To find who's the tallest,
We start with the smallest . . .

> We start with the smallest. Then what do we do?
> We line them all up. Back to back. Two by two.
> Taller and taller. And, when we are through,
> We finally will find one who's taller than who.

But you have to be smart and keep watching their feet.
Because sometimes they stand on their tiptoes and cheat.

And so, from the smaller, we stack 'em up taller
And taller. And taller. And taller and taller.
And now! Here's the one who is taller than all-er!
He's yours. He's all yours. He's the very top tallest.
I know you'll enjoy him. The tallest of all-est!

I'll have him shipped home to you, Birthday Express.
That costs quite a lot. But I couldn't care less.
Today is your birthday! Today You are You!
So what if it costs me a thousand or two.

Today is your birthday! You get what you wish.
You also might like a nice Time-Telling Fish.

So I'll send Diver Getz and I'll send Diver Gitz
Deep under the sea in their undersea kits.
In all the wide world there are no better pets
Than the Time-Telling Fish that Gitz gits and Getz gets.

But, speaking of time . . .
Why, good gracious alive!
That Time-Telling Fish says it's quarter to five!
I had no idea it was getting so late!
We have to get going! We have a big date!

And so, as the sunset burns red in the west,
Comes the night of the Day-of-the-Best-of-the-Best!
The Night-of-All-Nights-of-All-Nights in Katroo!
So, according to rule, what we usually do
Is saddle up two Hooded Klopfers named Alice
And gallop like mad to the Birthday Pal-alace.
Your Big Birthday Party soon starts to begin
In the finest Pal-alace you've ever been in!

Now this Birthday Pal-alace, as soon you will see,
Has exactly nine thousand, four hundred and three
Rooms to play games in! Twelve halls for brass bands!
Not counting the fifty-three hamburger stands.
And besides all of that, there are sixty-five rooms
Just for keeping the Sweeping-Up-Afterwards-Brooms.
Because, after your party, as well you may guess,
It will take twenty days just to sweep up the mess.

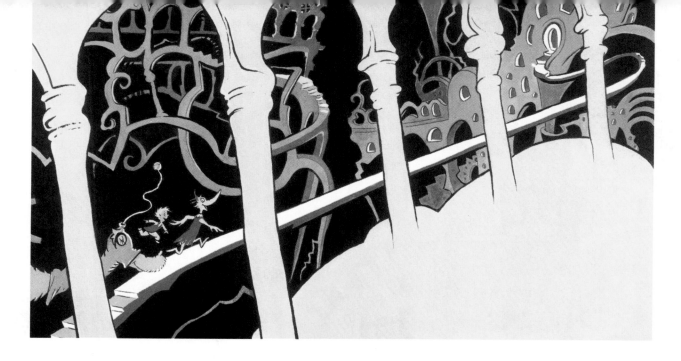

First, we're greeted by Drummers who drum as they come.
And next come the Strummers who strum as they come.
And the Drummers who drum and Strummers who strum
Are followed by Zummers who come as they zum.
Just look at those Zummers! They're sort of like Plumbers.
They come along humming, with heads in their plumbing
And that makes the music that Zummers call zumming!

And all of this beautiful zumming and humming
And plumbing and strumming and drumming and coming . . .
All of it, all of it,
All is for you!

LOOK!
    Dr. Derring's Singing Herrings!
    Derrings Singing, Spelling Herrings!
    See what Derring's Herrings do!
    They sing and spell it! All for you!

And here comes your cake! Cooked by Snookers and Snookers,
The Official Katroo Happy Birthday Cake Cookers.
And Snookers and Snookers, I'm happy to say,
Are the only cake cookers who cook cakes today
Made of guaranteed, certified strictly Grade-A
Peppermint cucumber sausage-paste butter!
And the world's finest cake slicers, Dutter and Dutter
And Dutter and Dutter, with hatchets a-flutter,
High up on the poop deck, stand ready to cut her.

228

Today you are you! That is truer than true!
There is no one alive who is you-er than you!
Shout loud, "I am lucky to be what I am!
Thank goodness I'm not just a clam or a ham
Or a dusty old jar of sour gooseberry jam!
I am what I am! That's a great thing to be!
If I say so myself, "HAPPY BIRTHDAY TO ME!"

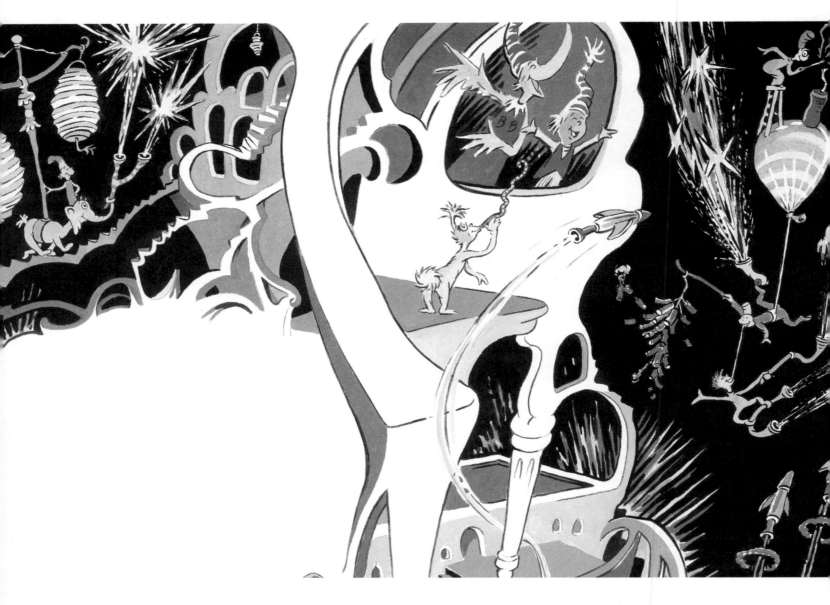

Now, by Horseback and Bird-back and Hiffer-back, too,
Come your friends! All your friends! From all over Katroo!
And the Birthday Pal-alace heats up with hot friends
And your party goes on!
On and on
Till it ends.

When it ends,
You're much happier,
Richer and fatter.
And the Bird flies you home
On a very soft platter.

So that's
What the Birthday Bird
Does in Katroo.

And I wish
I could do
All these great things for *you!*

Seuss covers for two humor magazines of the 1930s.

BIRDS ON THE BRAIN

The Great Birthday Bird was just one of many birds that began appearing in Ted Geisel's art almost from the time he started drawing. Perhaps he harbored a secret wish to fly, though some of his birds seem a bit too heavy to get off the ground!

"DARLING—WITH CONDITIONS AS THEY ARE, WE'VE SIMPLY GOT TO LET THE CANARY GO!"

Two paintings from a printer's promotional calendar, circa 1935.

"IT'S OUR FIRST . . . DON'T YOU THINK IT LOOKS LIKE GEORGE?"

Gertrude McFuzz from *Yertle the Turtle and Other Stories,* 1958.

"It's hard to believe, but this bird called the Pelf *lays eggs that are three times as big as herself!*" from *Scrambled Eggs Super!,* 1953.

Horton hatches an Elephant-Bird, from *Horton Hatches the Egg,* 1940.

Untitled and undated oil on canvas from Ted's personal collection.

we love sam

The familiar words of a beloved book from early childhood strike a chord deep within us that is like no other. Whether we are instantly transported to an old house in Paris or a great green room, we are infused with the memories those lines evoke on a cellular level. The only more vivid, enduring literary memory of young children is the first words they are able to read themselves.

As a child, beginning school in 1960, I distinctly recall opening my first-grade reader and recognizing the word *look*. Though my classmates and I were bored by the stories of those texts, we were thrilled with the process of reading. By the time my brother started school three years later, things had changed dramatically. He entered kindergarten able to read after a few encounters with *The Cat in the Hat* and a steady diet of *Green Eggs and Ham*.

As a children's librarian, I came to recognize *Green Eggs and Ham* as the quintessential book for beginning readers. Challenged by his publisher, Bennett Cerf, Dr. Seuss composed the book with a mere fifty words, winning their fifty-dollar bet. Forty-nine of those carefully chosen words consist of only one syllable, providing a perfect training ground for emergent readers. Young children can depend on the rhyme pattern and visual clues in the illustrations to maintain their interest and provide them with the illusion of reading. The structure and repetition build confidence among the book's listeners and spark

a natural introduction to wordplay as children extend the experience with adults' help, searching for their own rhymes in the same beguiling rhythm. In my library work, parents sometimes sigh and bemoan the number of times the book is read daily in their household. I cheerily and resolutely remark on their luck at having children with such good taste, and suggest that a child's request for repeated readings is really like a parent's desire to hear a favorite song over and over.

As a parent, I had my own taste of the *Green Eggs and Ham* phenomenon, but at least I had the satisfaction of discovering that I had been right about its perfection all along. The real brilliance, I realized, lies in the humor and the playfulness of the plot. And kids can't resist the fact that the patient persistence of a small, congenial character (who is also right) ultimately leads to the enlightenment and conversion of an impatient, stubborn, larger character. These are the elements that lead us back to the text repeatedly and that have firmly established its position in the pop culture of multiple generations. Readers of all ages have committed it to memory and can recite it at the drop of a hat, from a graduating class at Princeton to a rap version on KALX (the radio station for the University of California at Berkeley) to a straight-faced reading by Jesse Jackson on *Saturday Night Live*.

Over the years I've often thought, is it a coincidence that my son is named Sam? Probably not!

STARR LaTRONICA

youth services manager, Four County Library System, N.Y.

green eggs
and ham

[ORIGINALLY PUBLISHED IN 1960]

That Sam-I-am!
That Sam-I-am!
I do not like
that Sam-I-am!

Do you like
green eggs and ham?

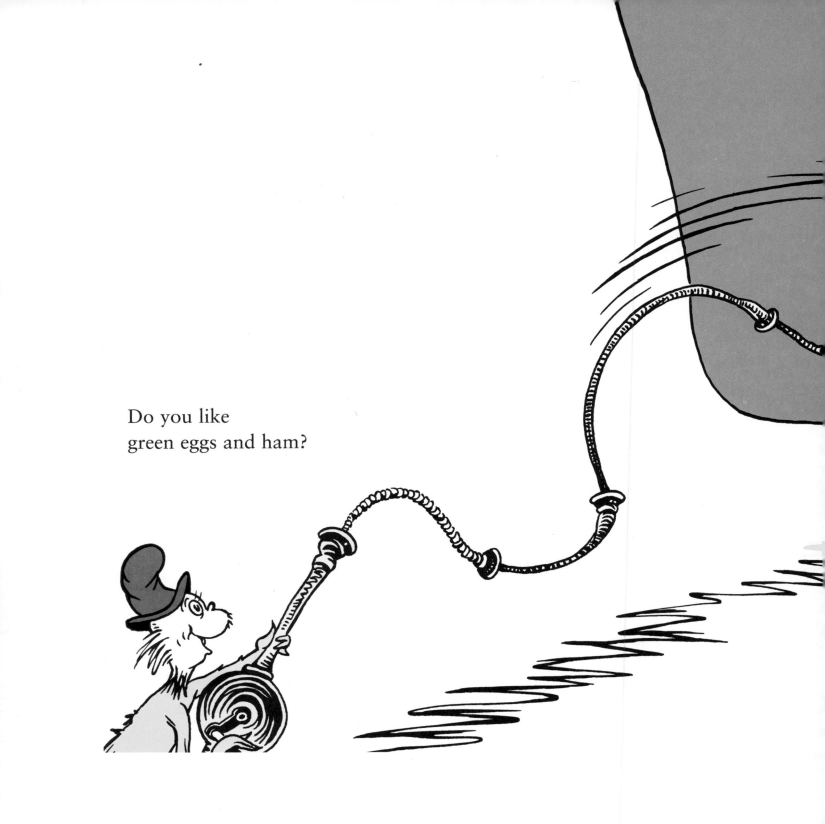

I do not like them,
Sam-I-am.
I do not like
green eggs and ham.

Would you like them
here or there?

I would not like them
here or there.
I would not like them
anywhere.
I do not like
green eggs and ham.
I do not like them,
Sam-I-am.

Would you like them
in a house?
Would you like them
with a mouse?

I do not like them
in a house.
I do not like them
with a mouse.
I do not like them
here or there.
I do not like them
anywhere.
I do not like green eggs and ham.
I do not like them, Sam-I-am.

Would you eat them
in a box?
Would you eat them
with a fox?

Not in a box.
Not with a fox.
Not in a house.
Not with a mouse.
I would not eat them here or there.
I would not eat them anywhere.
I would not eat green eggs and ham.
I do not like them, Sam-I-am.

Would you? Could you?
In a car?
Eat them! Eat them!
Here they are.

I would not,
could not,
in a car.

You may like them.
You will see.
You may like them
in a tree!

I would not, could not, in a tree.
Not in a car! You let me be.

I do not like them in a box.
I do not like them with a fox.
I do not like them in a house.
I do not like them with a mouse.
I do not like them here or there.
I do not like them anywhere.
I do not like green eggs and ham.
I do not like them, Sam-I-am.

A train! A train!
A train! A train!
Could you, would you,
on a train?

Not on a train! Not in a tree!
Not in a car! Sam! Let me be!

I would not, could not, in a box.
I could not, would not, with a fox.
I will not eat them with a mouse.
I will not eat them in a house.
I will not eat them here or there.
I will not eat them anywhere.
I do not eat green eggs and ham.
I do not like them, Sam-I-am.

Say!
In the dark?
Here in the dark!
Would you, could you, in the dark?

I would not, could not,
in the dark.

Would you, could you,
in the rain?

I would not, could not, in the rain.
Not in the dark. Not on a train.
Not in a car. Not in a tree.
I do not like them, Sam, you see.
Not in a house. Not in a box.
Not with a mouse. Not with a fox.
I will not eat them here or there.
I do not like them anywhere!

You do not like
green eggs and ham?

I do not
like them,
Sam-I-am.

Could you, would you,
with a goat?

I would not,
could not,
with a goat!

253

Would you, could you,
on a boat?

I could not, would not, on a boat.
I will not, will not, with a goat.
I will not eat them in the rain.
I will not eat them on a train.
Not in the dark! Not in a tree!
Not in a car! You let me be!

I do not like them in a box.
I do not like them with a fox.
I will not eat them in a house.
I do not like them with a mouse.
I do not like them here or there.
I do not like them ANYWHERE!

I do not like
green eggs
and ham!

I do not like them,
Sam-I-am.

You do not like them.
So you say.
Try them! Try them!
And you may.
Try them and you may, I say.

Sam!
If you will let me be,
I will try them.
You will see.

Say!
I like green eggs and ham!
I do! I like them, Sam-I-am!
And I would eat them in a boat.
And I would eat them with a goat...

And I will eat them in the rain.
And in the dark. And on a train.
And in a car. And in a tree.
They are so good, so good, you see!

So I will eat them in a box.
And I will eat them with a fox.
And I will eat them in a house.
And I will eat them with a mouse.
And I will eat them here and there.
Say! I will eat them ANYWHERE!

I do so like
green eggs and ham!
Thank you!
Thank you,
Sam-I-am!

HOW TO WHIP UP GREEN EGGS AND HAM

These color sketches for the cover (top left) and interior spreads of Dr. Seuss's Beginner Book classic Green Eggs and Ham *offer a fascinating window into Ted's creative process. He blocked out each spread using colored pencil and crayon and taped down cut-out pieces of his typewritten manuscript. This showed him how the text and pictures were working together. Note the changes in the final book, most notably on the top spread (see page 243) in which the narrator now faces Sam-I-Am and stands out against a Seussian aqua. Ted often had trouble nailing down the cover, and this book was no exception. The final cover shows only the narrator and the green eggs and ham, and the pale yellow background becomes a neon orange. The selling point "A 50 Word Book" also didn't make it to the final cover, although it was indeed a well-deserved boast.*

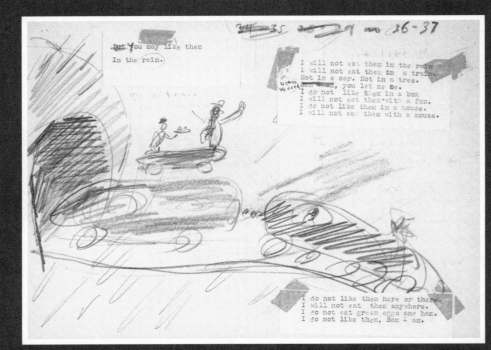

he taught us how to think

The Sneetches first appeared in 1961, about a year after I first appeared. I do not remember how old I was when I first heard the story—probably four or five—but I do remember that it made a very strong impression on my young mind. "How silly," I thought. "How silly that anyone would think they were better because they had a star on their belly!" I did not consciously relate this hilarious, endearing tale to the struggle for civil rights, which I was beginning to hear about on the nightly news, but when I look back now, I realize that it was this deceptively simple story that helped shape my views on intolerance and racism. So brilliantly had Dr. Seuss written this story that, as a child and teenager, I couldn't even understand how someone could be a bigot. How could anyone dislike someone else simply because of the color of their skin or the shape of their eyes or the country they came from? It seemed to me they would have to be as foolish and stupid as a Sneetch to think that way.

I was fortunate enough to meet Ted Geisel a few times. He was every bit as charming, clever, and delightful as you would expect. The first time we met, I said, "You taught me how to read!" Without a moment's hesitation, he replied, "Funny, I don't remember doing that." Well, when you've played straight man to Dr. Seuss, you know you've arrived!

But the truth is that Dr. Seuss taught millions of children not only to read, but to think. And he taught us—not through fear and warnings, but through joy and laughter—that what makes us different on the outside is not important. It's what we share on the inside that makes us all special. For in one way or another, we're all Sneetches. And that old con artist Sylvester McMonkey McBean is still wrong—for Dr. Seuss proved that you *can* teach a Sneetch!

PETER GLASSMAN

founder of Books of Wonder,
New York City's oldest independent children's bookstore

the sneetches

[ORIGINALLY PUBLISHED IN 1961]

Now, the Star-Belly Sneetches
Had bellies with stars.
The Plain-Belly Sneetches
Had none upon thars.

Those stars weren't so big. They were really so small
You might think such a thing wouldn't matter at all.

But, because they had stars, all the Star-Belly Sneetches
Would brag, "We're the best kind of Sneetch on the beaches."
With their snoots in the air, they would sniff and they'd snort
"We'll have nothing to do with the Plain-Belly sort!"
And whenever they met some, when they were out walking,
They'd hike right on past them without even talking.

When the Star-Belly children went out to play ball,
Could a Plain Belly get in the game . . . ? Not at all.
You only could play if your bellies had stars
And the Plain-Belly children had none upon thars.

When the Star-Belly Sneetches had frankfurter roasts
Or picnics or parties or marshmallow toasts,
They never invited the Plain-Belly Sneetches.
They left them out cold, in the dark of the beaches.
They kept them away. Never let them come near.
And that's how they treated them year after year.

Then ONE day, it seems . . . while the Plain-Belly Sneetches
Were moping and doping alone on the beaches,
Just sitting there wishing their bellies had stars . . .
A stranger zipped up in the strangest of cars!

"My friends," he announced in a voice clear and keen,
"My name is Sylvester McMonkey McBean.
And I've heard of your troubles. I've heard you're unhappy.
But I can fix that. I'm the Fix-it-Up Chappie.
I've come here to help you. I have what you need.
And my prices are low. And I work at great speed.
And my work is one hundred per cent guaranteed!"

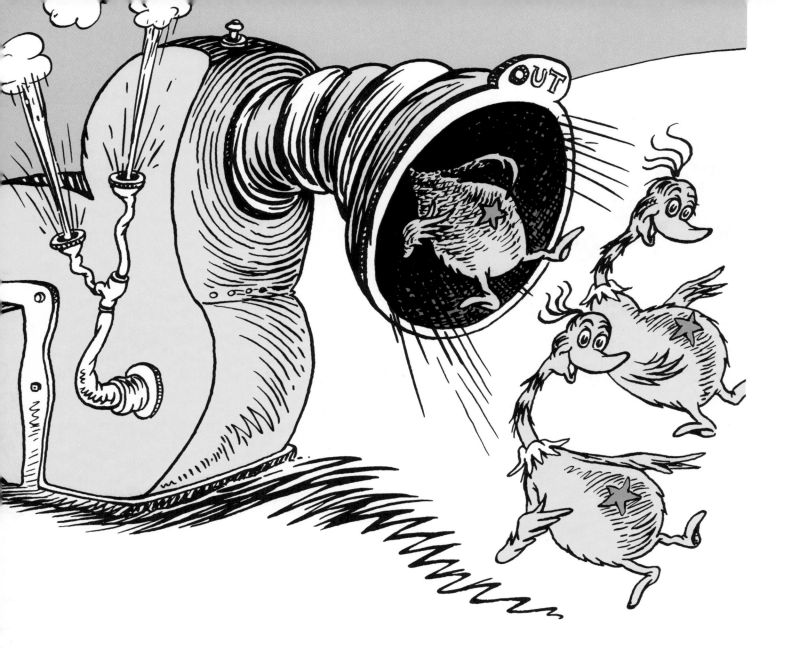

Then, quickly, Sylvester McMonkey McBean
Put together a very peculiar machine.
And he said, "You want stars like a Star-Belly Sneetch . . . ?
My friends, you can have them for three dollars each!"

"Just pay me your money and hop right aboard!"
So they clambered inside. Then the big machine roared
And it klonked. And it bonked. And it jerked. And it berked
And it bopped them about. But the thing really worked!
When the Plain-Belly Sneetches popped out, they had stars!
They actually did. They had stars upon thars!

Then they yelled at the ones who had stars at the start,
"We're exactly like you! You can't tell us apart.
We're all just the same, now, you snooty old smarties!
And now we can go to your frankfurter parties."

"Good grief!" groaned the ones who had stars at the first.
"We're *still* the best Sneetches and they are the worst.
But, now, how in the world will we know," they all frowned,
"If which kind is what, or the other way round?"

Then up came McBean with a very sly wink
And he said, "Things are not quite as bad as you think.
So you don't know who's who. That is perfectly true.
But come with me, friends. Do you know what I'll do?
I'll make you, again, the best Sneetches on beaches
And all it will cost you is ten dollars eaches."

"Belly stars are no longer in style," said McBean.
"What you need is a trip through my Star-*Off* Machine.
This wondrous contraption will take *off* your stars
So you won't look like Sneetches who have them on thars."
And that handy machine
Working very precisely
Removed all the stars from their tummies quite nicely.

Then, with snoots in the air, they paraded about
And they opened their beaks and they let out a shout,
"We know who is who! Now there isn't a doubt.
The best kind of Sneetches are Sneetches without!"

Then, of course, those with stars all got frightfully mad.
To be wearing a star now was frightfully bad.
Then, of course, old Sylvester McMonkey McBean
Invited *them* into his Star-Off Machine.

Then, of course from THEN on, as you probably guess,
Things really got into a horrible mess.

All the rest of that day, on those wild screaming beaches,
The Fix-it-Up Chappie kept fixing up Sneetches.
Off again! On again!
In again! Out again!
Through the machines they raced round and about again,
Changing their stars every minute or two.
They kept paying money. They kept running through
Until neither the Plain nor the Star-Bellies knew
Whether this one was that one . . . or that one was this one
Or which one was what one . . . or what one was who.

Then, when every last cent
Of their money was spent,
The Fix-it-Up Chappie packed up
And he went.

And he laughed as he drove
In his car up the beach,
"They never will learn.
No. You can't teach a Sneetch!"

But McBean was quite wrong. I'm quite happy to say
That the Sneetches got really quite smart on that day,
The day they decided that Sneetches are Sneetches
And no kind of Sneetch is the best on the beaches.
That day, all the Sneetches forgot about stars
And whether they had one, or not, upon thars.

From *Oh, the Thinks You Can Think!*, 1975.

The Triple-Sling Jigger and the Jigger-Rock Snatchem from *The Butter Battle Book*, 1984.

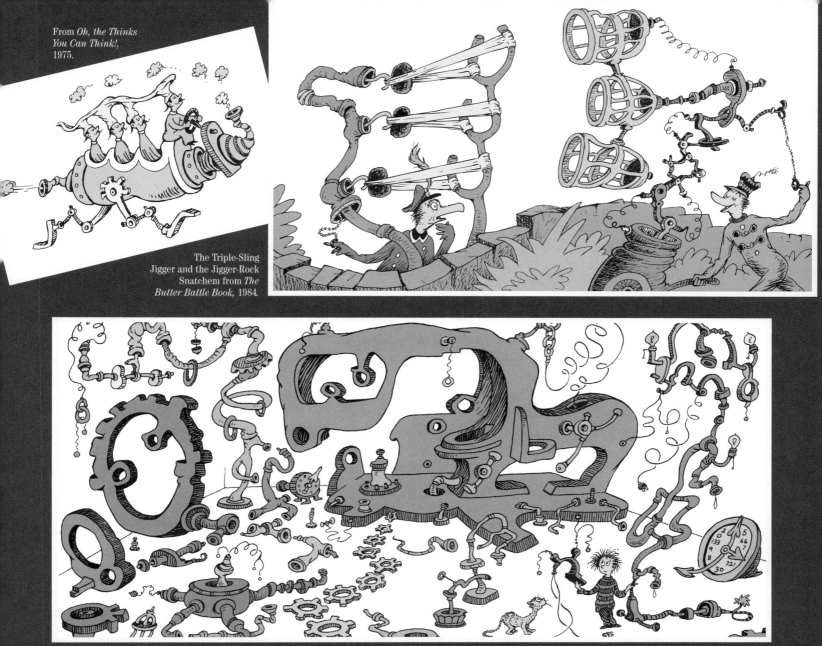

Herbie Hart, who has taken his Throm-dim-bu-lator apart, from *Did I Ever Tell You How Lucky You Are?*, 1973.

From *You're Only Old Once!*, 1986.

MACHINES WITHOUT PATENTS

Sylvester McMonkey McBean's Star-On and Star-Off Sneetch machines are just two of the many contraptions invented by Ted Geisel. Though he possessed a notable lack of engineering skills (his wife Audrey once said that he couldn't even fix a running toilet by jiggling the handle), many of his books indicate that he was fascinated by machines. It seems likely that he was influenced by the cartoonist Rube Goldberg's absurdly complex machines that made simple tasks difficult. It seems even more certain that Ted's Sneetch machines were inspired by the advertisement he created in 1934 for Daggett & Ramsdell toiletries (pictured at right).

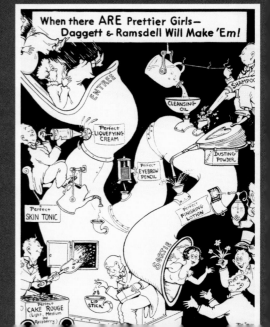

looks like something from seuss!

Sure, Seuss was the master of clever verse, but can we talk about that equally clever, strange, surreal, masterful Seuss artwork? Where did it come from? What kind of twisted bean could create such fantastic creatures as the Collapsible Frink, those two Foona-Lagoona Baboona, that pair of Offt (sleeping aloft), and others in *Dr. Seuss's Sleep Book?*

Seuss's books never disappoint visually. Look at that fanciful flora and crazed architecture. They may seem to have sprung solely from Seuss's imagination, but when we learn that extensive travels took him to exotic locales like Peru, Cambodia, Casablanca, and Fez, we gain some insight into the origins of the Truffula Tree or those strange, Mediterranean-style houses of Solla Sollew.

Poring over the books, I always find new surprises. In *If I Ran the Circus,* I just came across a spread of unusual restraint in the Seuss canon (no, it's not the one of the creature being shot from the cannon). It's the Juggling Jott, who is seen juggling twenty-two question marks. He appears in a single white spotlight. He is surrounded by spectators who are all rendered in an uncomplicated ink-line over a solid background of 100 percent cyan blue. It's stunning in its simplicity.

If you look at the books in the order in which they were published, you see a variety of styles and experimentation, and yet all remain consistently "Seuss." His first book, *And to Think That I Saw It on Mulberry Street,* has a graphic-comic-strip look. Next, there was a period of crayon with wash. But before settling into the classic pen-and-ink look that most of us identify with him comes what, in my opinion, is his most handsome book, *McElligot's Pool,* Seuss's

first Caldecott Honor Book. It's bursting with watercolor. It has a sophisticated palette and confident brushstrokes. There are quiet pages and others packed with detail. (I counted sixty-nine fish on the last spread alone.)

Judith and Neil Morgan wrote in *Dr. Seuss & Mr. Geisel* that *McElligot's Pool* was his only book in watercolor because "he decided that children prefer flat, bold colors and cartoon illustrations." This is too bad. It would have been a treat to see more books in this style. It's also not entirely accurate. Though not as elaborate as *McElligot's Pool, Happy Birthday to You!* and *I Can Lick 30 Tigers Today!* are also fun watercolor detours.

Later, though his line became looser and scratchier (starting around the time of *Did I Ever Tell You How Lucky You Are?*), he continued to experiment with color and subtle printing techniques. He was always trying new things and expanding visual boundaries.

As an illustrator, I find it interesting that Dr. Seuss had no imitators. That's unusual in the world of children's books. On any library shelf you're sure to find illustrators "attempting" Beatrix Potter or Maurice Sendak or Chris Van Allsburg—but never Seuss. It can't be done.

In 1998, I had the honor of illustrating the posthumous Seuss text completed by Jack Prelutsky, *Hooray for Diffendoofer Day!* One of the benefits of the project was a chance to visit the Seuss house in La Jolla, California. Inside a Mediterranean tower that looked like it had come from one of his books, I saw a terrarium of unusual, exotic orchids. I couldn't help saying to Audrey Geisel what most of us have said at one time or another, "This looks like something from Seuss!"

LANE SMITH

Caldecott Honor Book illustrator of
The Stinky Cheese Man and Other Fairly Stupid Tales

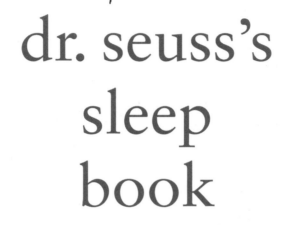

dr. seuss's
sleep
book

[ORIGINALLY PUBLISHED IN 1962]

The news
Just came in
From the County of Keck
That a very small bug
By the name of Van Vleck
Is yawning so wide
You can look down his neck.

This may not seem
Very important, I know.
But it *is*. So I'm bothering
Telling you so.

A yawn is quite catching, you see. Like a cough.
It just takes one yawn to start other yawns off.
NOW the news has come in that some friends of Van Vleck's
Are yawning so wide you can look down *their* necks.

At this moment, right now,
Under seven more noses,
Great yawns are in blossom.
They're blooming like roses.

The yawn of that one little bug is still spreading!
According to latest reports, it is heading
Across the wide fields, through the sleepy night air,
Across the whole country toward every-which-where.
And people are gradually starting to say,
"I feel rather drowsy. I've had quite a day."

Creatures are starting to
    think about rest.
Two Biffer-Baum Birds are
    now building their nest.
They do it each night.
    And quite often I wonder
How they do this big job
    without making a blunder.

But that is *their* problem.
Not yours. And not mine.
The point is: They're going to bed.
And that's fine.

Sleep thoughts
Are spreading
Throughout the whole land.
The time for night-brushing of teeth is at hand.
Up at Herk-Heimer Falls, where the great river rushes
And crashes down crags in great gargling gushes,
The Herk-Heimer Sisters are using their brushes.
Those falls are just grand for tooth-brushing beneath
If you happen to be up that way with your teeth.

The news just came in from the Castle of Krupp
That the lights are all out and the drawbridge is up.
And the old drawbridge draw-er just said with a yawn,
"My drawbridge is drawn and it's going to stay drawn

'Til the milkman delivers the milk, about dawn.
I'm going to bed now. So nobody better
Come round with a special delivery letter."

The number
Of sleepers
Is steadily growing.
Bed is where
More and more people are going.
In Culpepper Springs, in the Stilt-Walkers' Hall,
The stilt-walkers' stilts are all stacked on the wall.
The stilt-walker walkers have called it a day.
They're all tuckered out and they're snoozing away.
This is very big news. It's important to know.
And that's why I'm bothering telling you so.

Way out in the west, in the town of Mercedd,
The Hinkle-Horn Honking Club just went to bed.
Every horn has been quietly hung on a hook,
For the night, in its own private Hinkle-Horn Nook.

All this long, happy day, they've been honking about
And the Hinkle-Horn Honkers have honked themselves out.
But they'll wake up quite fresh in the morning. And then . . .
They'll start right in Hinkle-Horn honking again.

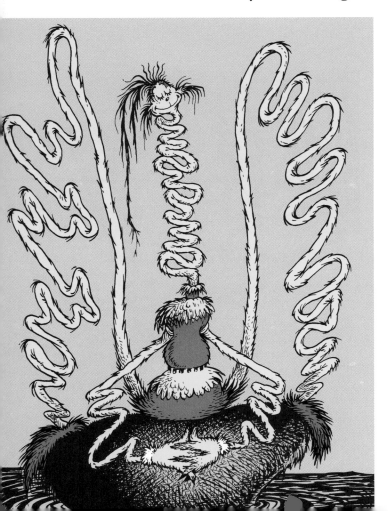

Everywhere, creatures
Are falling asleep.
The Collapsible Frink
Just collapsed in a heap.
And, by adding the Frink
To the others before,
I am able to give you
The Who's-Asleep-Score:
Right now, forty thousand
Four hundred and four
Creatures are happily,
Deeply in slumber.
I think you'll agree
That's a whopping fine number.

Counting up sleepers . . ?
Just how do we do it . . ?
Really quite simple. There's nothing much to it.
We find out how many, we learn the amount
By an Audio-Telly-o-Tally-o Count.
On a mountain, halfway between Reno and Rome,
We have a machine in a plexiglass dome
Which listens and looks into everyone's home.
And whenever it sees a new sleeper go flop,
It jiggles and lets a new Biggel-Ball drop.
Our chap counts these balls as they plup in a cup.
And that's how we know who is down and who's up.

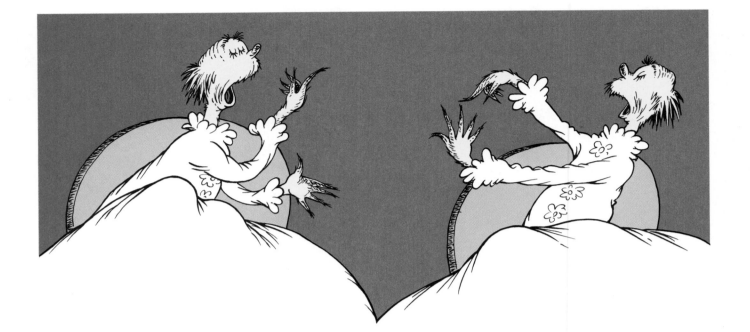

Do you talk in your sleep . . ?
It's a wonderful sport
And I have some news of this sport to report.
The World-Champion Sleep-Talkers, Jo and Mo Redd-Zoff,
Have just gone to sleep and they're talking their heads off.
For fifty-five years, now, each chattering brother
Has babbled and gabbled all night to the other.

They've talked about laws and they've talked about gauze.
They've talked about paws and they've talked about flaws.
They've talked quite a lot about old Santa Claus.
And the reason I'm telling you this is because
You should take up this sport. It's just fine for the jaws.

Do you walk in your sleep . . ?
I just had a report
Of some interesting news of this popular sport.
Near Finnigan Fen, there's a sleepwalking group
Which not only walks, but it walks a-la-hoop!
Every night they go miles. Why, they walk to such length
They have to keep eating to keep up their strength.

So, every so often, one puts down his hoop,
Stops hooping and does some quick snooping for soup.
That's why they are known as the Hoop-Soup-Snoop Group.

Sleepwalking, too, are the Curious Crandalls
Who sleepwalk on hills with assorted-sized candles.
The Crandalls walk nightly in slumbering peace
In spite of slight burns from the hot dripping grease.
The Crandalls wear candles because they walk far
And, if they wake up,
Want to see where they are.

Now the news has arrived
From the Valley of Vail
That a Chippendale Mupp has just bitten his tail,
Which he does every night before shutting his eyes.
Such nipping sounds silly. But, really, it's wise.

He has no alarm clock. So this is the way
  He makes sure that he'll wake at the right time of day.
   His tail is so long, he won't feel any pain
     'Til the nip makes the trip and gets up to his brain.
      In exactly eight hours, the Chippendale Mupp
        Will, at last, feel the bite and yell "Ouch!" and wake up.

      A Mr. and Mrs. J. Carmichael Krox
        Have just gone to bed near the town of Fort Knox.
          And they, by the way, have the finest of clocks.

I'm not at all sure that I quite quite understand
Just how the thing works, with that one extra hand.
But I *do* know this clock does one very slick trick.
It doesn't tick tock. How it goes, is tock tick.
So, with ticks in its tocker, and tocks in its ticker
It saves lots of time and the sleepers sleep quicker.

What a fine night for sleeping! From all that I hear,
It's the best night for sleeping in many a year.
They're even asleep in the Zwieback Motel!
And people don't usually sleep there too well.

The beds are like rocks and, as everyone knows,
The sheets are too short. They won't cover your toes.
SO, if people are actually sleeping in THERE . . .
It's a great night for sleeping! It must be the air.

293

It's a great night for snores! I just had a report
Of some boys who are tops in this musical sport.
The snortiest snorers in all our fair land
Are Snorter McPhail and his Snore-a-Snort Band.
This band can snore *Dixie* and old *Swanee River*
So loud it would make forty elephants shiver.

The loudest of all of the boys is McPhail.
HE snores with his head in a three-gallon pail.
So they snore in a cave twenty miles out of town.
If they snored closer in, they would snore the town down.

Do you know who's asleep
Out in Foona-Lagoona..?
Two very nice
Foona-Lagoona Baboona.

We've added them into our Who's-Asleep Count
Which has grown to a really amazing amount.
Exactly eight million, eight hundred and eight
Creatures are sleeping now! Isn't that great!

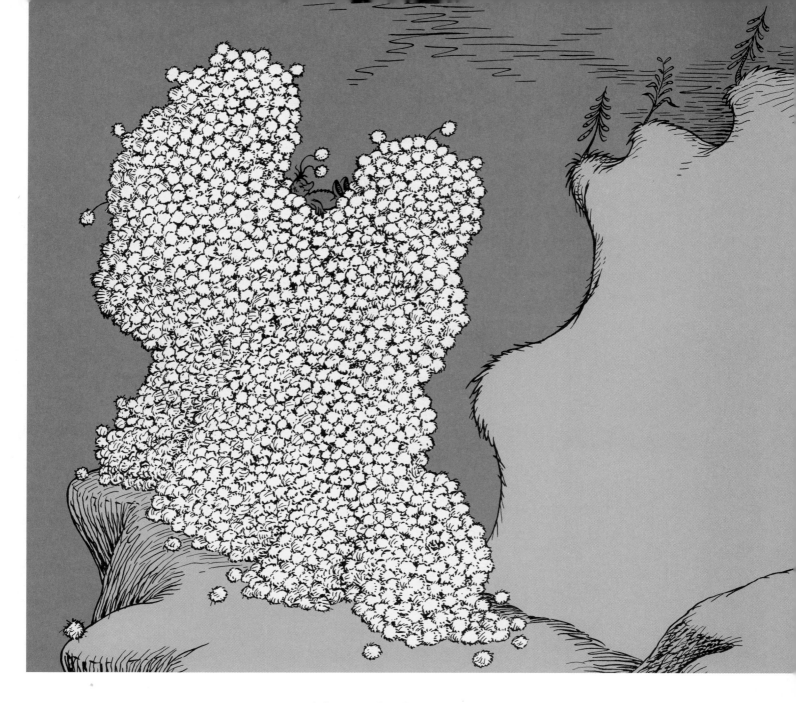

A Jedd is in bed,
And the bed of a Jedd
Is the softest
Of beds in the world,
It is said.
He makes it from pom poms
He grows on his head.
And he's sleeping right now
On the softest of fluff,
Completely exhausted
From growing the stuff.

The news has come in from the District of Dofft
That two Offt are asleep and they're sleeping aloft.
And how are they able to sleep off the ground..?
I'll tell you. I weighed one last week and I found
That an Offt is SO light he weighs minus one pound!

A moose is asleep.
He is dreaming of moose drinks.
A goose is asleep.
He is dreaming of goose drinks.
That's well and good when a moose dreams of moose juice.
And nothing goes wrong when a goose dreams of goose juice.

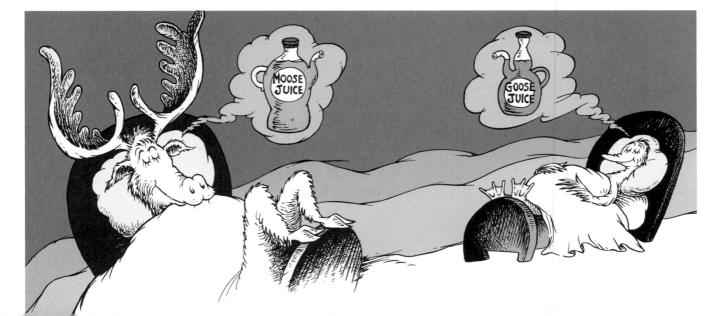

But it isn't too good when a moose and a goose
Start dreaming they're drinking the other one's juice.
Moose juice, not goose juice, is juice for a moose
And goose juice, not moose juice, is juice for a goose.
So, when goose gets a mouthful of juices of moose's
And moose gets a mouthful of juices of goose's,
They always fall out of their beds screaming screams.
SO . . .
I'm warning you, now! Never drink in your dreams.

Speaking of dreaming,
I think you should note
That the Bumble-Tub Club is now dreaming afloat.
Every night they go dreaming down Bumble-Tub Creek
Except for one night, every third or fourth week,
When they stop for repairs. 'Cause their bumble-tubs leak.
But tonight they're afloat, full of dreams, full of bliss,
And that's why I'm bothering telling you this.

At the fork of a road
In the Vale of Va-Vode
Five foot-weary salesmen have laid down their load.
All day they've raced round in the heat, at top speeds,
Unsuccessfully trying to sell Zizzer-Zoof Seeds
Which nobody wants because nobody needs.

Tomorrow will come. They'll go back to their chore.
They'll start on the road, Zizzer-Zoofing once more
But tonight they've forgotten their feet are so sore.
And that's what the wonderful night time is for.

Everywhere,
Creatures
Have shut off their voices.
They've all gone to bed
In the beds of their choices.

They're sleeping in bushes. They're sleeping in crannies.
Some on their stomachs, and some on their fannies.
They're peacefully sleeping in comfortable holes.
Some, even, on soft-tufted barber shop poles.
The number of sleepers is now past the millions!
The number of sleepers is now in the billions!
They're sleeping on steps! And on strings! And on floors!

In mailboxes, ships, and the keyholes of doors!
Every worm on a fishhook is safe for the night.
Every fish in the sea is too sleepy to bite.
Every whale in the ocean has turned off his spout.
Every light between here and Far Foodle is out.
And now, adding things up, we are way beyond billions!
Our Who's-Asleep-Score is now up in the Zillions!

Ninety-nine zillion,
Nine trillion and two
Creatures are sleeping!
So . . .
How about you?

When you put out *your* light,
Then the number will be
Ninety-nine zillion
Nine trillion and three.

Good night.

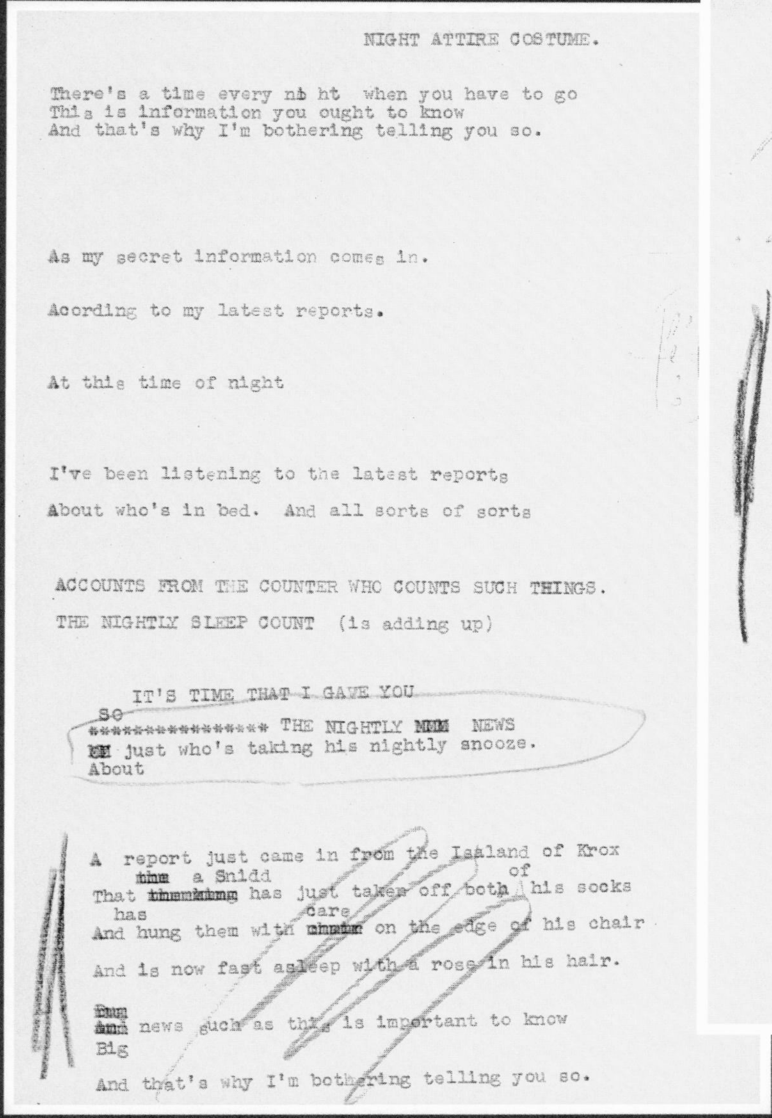

NIGHT ATTIRE COSTUME.

There's a time every night when you have to go
This is information you ought to know
And that's why I'm bothering telling you so.

As my secret information comes in.

Acording to my latest reports.

At this time of night

I've been listening to the latest reports
About who's in bed. And all sorts of sorts

ACCOUNTS FROM THE COUNTER WHO COUNTS SUCH THINGS.

THE NIGHTLY SLEEP COUNT (is adding up)

        IT'S TIME THAT I GAVE YOU
So
*************** THE NIGHTLY MEN NEWS
Of just who's taking his nightly snooze.
About

A report just came in from the Isaland of Krox
        a Snidd   of
That thinking has just taken off both his socks
    has   care
And hung them with mmmm on the edge of his chair
And is now fast asleep with a rose in his hair.

Big
news such as this is important to know
Big
And that's why I'm bothering telling you so.

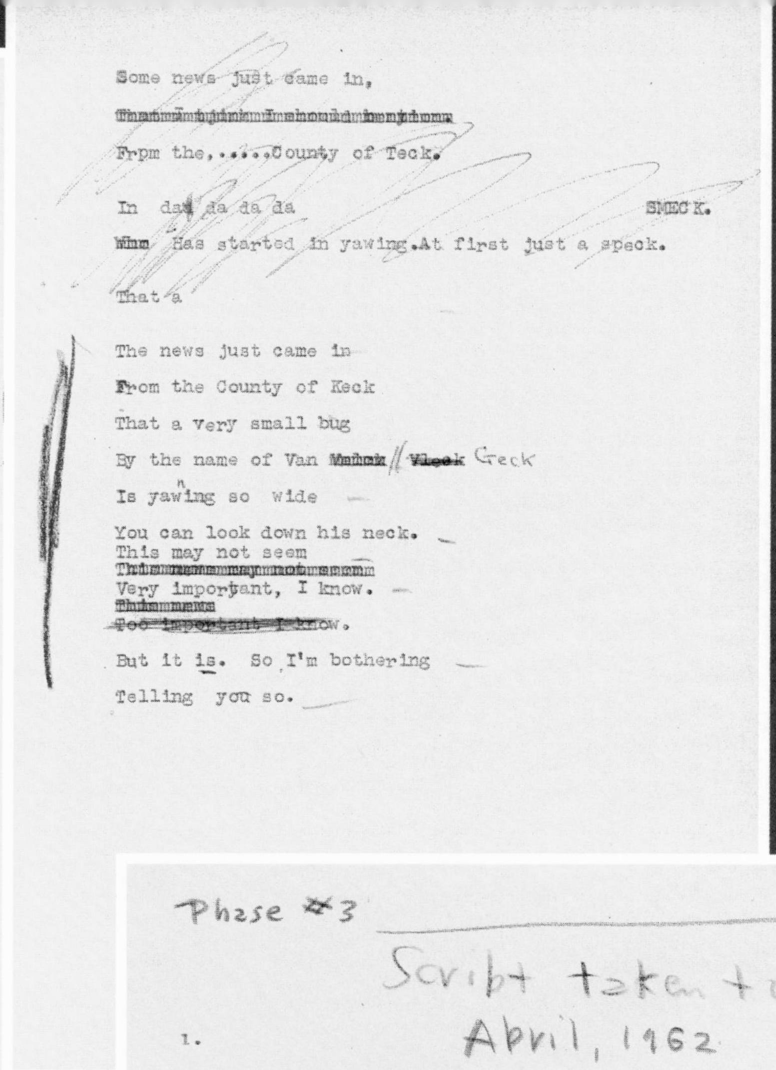

Some news just came in,

Frpm the,.....County of Teck.

In da da da da   SMECK.
Has started in yawing.At first just a speck.

That a

The news just came in

From the County of Keck

That a very small bug

By the name of Van Vleck Geck

Is yawing so wide

You can look down his neck.
This may not seem

Very important, I know.

Too important I know.

But it is. So I'm bothering

Telling you so.

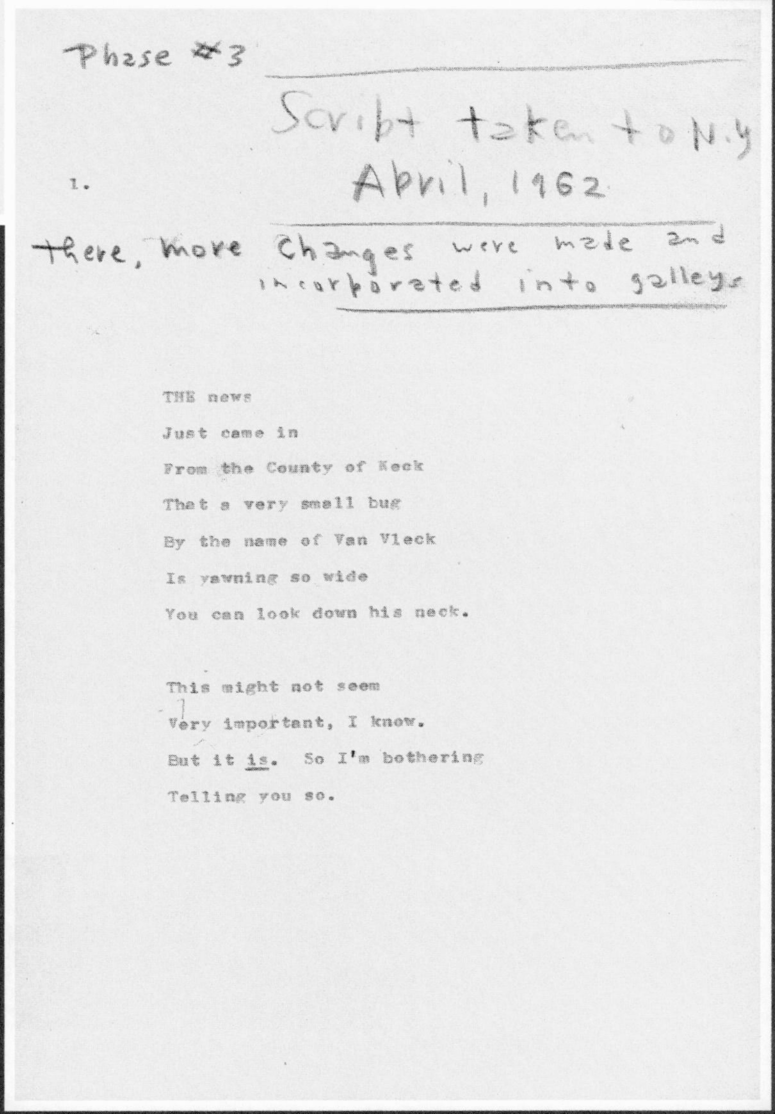

Phase #3

Script taken to N.Y
        April, 1962

1.

There, more changes were made and
        incorporated into galleys

THE news
Just came in
From the County of Keck
That a very small bug
By the name of Van Vleck
Is yawing so wide
You can look down his neck.

This might not seem
Very important, I know.
But it is. So I'm bothering
Telling you so.

IF AT FIRST YOU DON'T SUCCEED . . .

Try, try, again. That is exactly what Ted Geisel did every time he sat down to write a new book. Pictured here are his first, second, and third drafts of the opening page of Dr. Seuss's Sleep Book. The first draft (above left) is scarcely more than a germ of an idea. His lines marked in red probably indicate that he thought they were on the right track. In the second draft (above right), Ted has found the rhyme and meter he wants. The red marks probably indicate that he read it aloud to hear where the heavy beat fell—consistently on the last syllable of each line. The third draft (right) is almost identical to what appears in the printed book; "might" in the second stanza changed to "may" in the final version. Ted often reverted to words he had deleted in earlier drafts. In the second draft, he crossed out "Van Vleck" in favor of "Van Geck," but then went back to "Van Vleck" in the final version. The notes on this draft are in Ted's own characteristic handwriting. Like many writers of Ted's vintage, he always used inexpensive yellow typing paper for his drafts.

love it or lose it

Dear Kids,

Beware! This book may change your life.

Picture yourself playing in a city park, or in your backyard, if you're lucky enough to have one. What do you see? A tree to climb. Birds in a nest. Flowers.

Now imagine all that taken away. There's a parking lot. And a factory with smokestacks. Try planting flowers in the cement. Or breathing fresh air under the smokestacks. The world will be like this . . . unless we can teach the kids of the world to love it before we lose it.

How can we do that? Dr. Seuss found a way: he gets us laughing, gets us interested in the story of the very greedy Once-ler, who cared only about money. But the Once-ler's happiness and success were short-lived. Even *he* came to realize that we don't really need Thneeds.

Dr. Seuss asks us to speak up for the trees, the water, and the air. If something wrong is being done to the environment, speak up as the Lorax did. Talk to your parents, your teachers, your legislators. Talk to *anyone* who will listen.

Just by looking outside, we can see that the world is still a beautiful place. But, as Dr. Seuss put it, it won't be . . .

UNLESS someone like you
cares a whole awful lot,
nothing is going to get better.
It's not.

The most important thing that you kids can do is to ask the right questions, the kind that make people think about why we are destroying our world. And maybe we'll all learn to laugh as we speak up for the Lorax and one-up the Once-lers in our neighborhood. For it's you kids who will get us to clean up the mess.

What mess? Turn the page and start!

PETE SEEGER

songwriter and social activist, together with the Environmental Club
of Our Lady of Lourdes High School, Poughkeepsie, New York

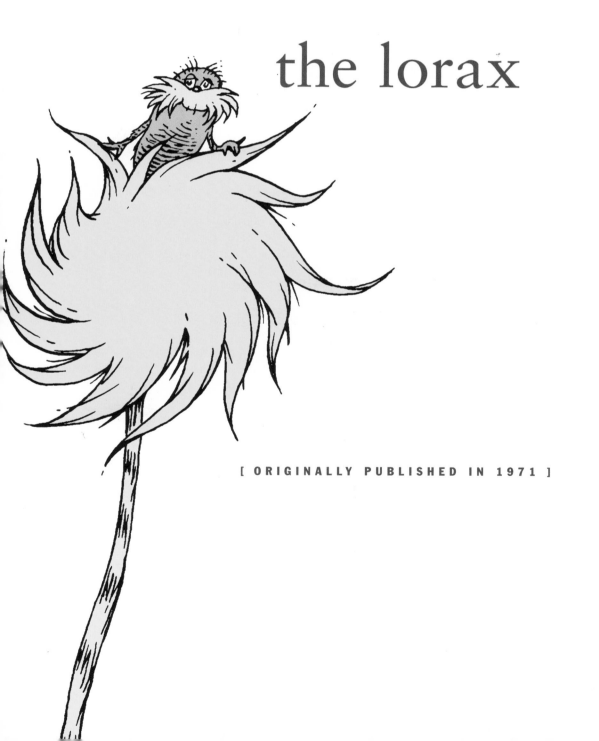

the lorax

[ORIGINALLY PUBLISHED IN 1971]

At the far end of town
where the Grickle-grass grows
and the wind smells slow-and-sour when it blows
and no birds ever sing excepting old crows . . .
is the Street of the Lifted Lorax.

And deep in the Grickle-grass, some people say,
if you look deep enough you can still see, today,
where the Lorax once stood
just as long as it could
before somebody lifted the Lorax away.

What *was* the Lorax?
And why was it there?
And why was it lifted and taken somewhere
from the far end of town where the Grickle-grass grows?
The old Once-ler still lives here.
Ask him. *He* knows.

You won't see the Once-ler.
Don't knock at his door.
He stays in his Lerkim on top of his store.
He lurks in his Lerkim, cold under the roof,
where he makes his own clothes
out of miff-muffered moof.
And on special dank midnights in August,
he peeks
out of the shutters
and sometimes he speaks
and tells how the Lorax was lifted away.

He'll tell you, perhaps . . .
if you're willing to pay.

On the end of a rope
he lets down a tin pail
and you have to toss in fifteen cents
and a nail
and the shell of a great-great-great-
grandfather snail.

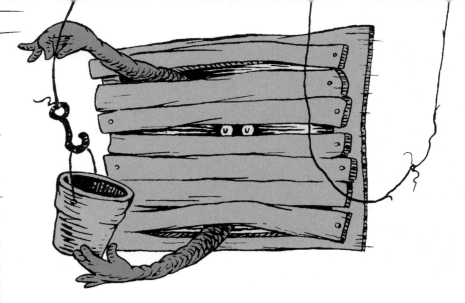

Then he pulls up the pail,
makes a most careful count
to see if you've paid him
the proper amount.

Then he hides what you paid him
away in his Snuvv,
his secret strange hole
in his gruvvulous glove.

Then he grunts, "I will call you by Whisper-ma-Phone,
for the secrets I tell are for your ears alone."

310

SLUPP!
Down slupps the Whisper-ma-Phone to your ear
and the old Once-ler's whispers are not very clear,
since they have to come down
through a snergelly hose,
and he sounds
as if he had
smallish bees up his nose.

"Now I'll tell you," he says, with his teeth sounding gray,
"how the Lorax got lifted and taken away...

 It all started way back...
 such a long, long time back...

Way back in the days when the grass was still green
and the pond was still wet
and the clouds were still clean,
and the song of the Swomee-Swans rang out in space . . .
one morning, I came to this glorious place.
And I first saw the trees!
The Truffula Trees!
The bright-colored tufts of the Truffula Trees!
Mile after mile in the fresh morning breeze.

And, under the trees, I saw Brown Bar-ba-loots
frisking about in their Bar-ba-loot suits
as they played in the shade and ate Truffula Fruits.

From the rippulous pond
came the comfortable sound
of the Humming-Fish humming
while splashing around.

But those *trees!* Those *trees!*
Those Truffula Trees!
All my life I'd been searching
for trees such as these.
The touch of their tufts
was much softer than silk.
And they had the sweet smell
of fresh butterfly milk.

I felt a great leaping
of joy in my heart.
I knew just what I'd do!
I unloaded my cart.

In no time at all, I had built a small shop.
Then I chopped down a Truffula Tree with one chop.
And with great skillful skill and with great speedy speed,
I took the soft tuft. And I knitted a Thneed!

The instant I'd finished, I heard a *ga-Zump!*
I looked.
I saw something pop out of the stump
of the tree I'd chopped down. It was sort of a man.
Describe him? . . . That's hard. I don't know if I can.

He was shortish. And oldish.
And brownish. And mossy.
And he spoke with a voice
that was sharpish and bossy.

"Mister!" he said with a sawdusty sneeze,
"I am the Lorax. I speak for the trees.
I speak for the trees, for the trees have no tongues.
And I'm asking you, sir, at the top of my lungs"—
he was very upset as he shouted and puffed—
"What's that THING you've made out of my Truffula tuft?"

"Look, Lorax," I said. "There's no cause for alarm.
I chopped just one tree. I am doing no harm.
I'm being quite useful. This thing is a Thneed.
A Thneed's a Fine-Something-That-All-People-Need!
It's a shirt. It's a sock. It's a glove. It's a hat.
But it has *other* uses. Yes, far beyond that.
You can use it for carpets. For pillows! For sheets!
Or curtains! Or covers for bicycle seats!"

> The Lorax said,
> "Sir! You are crazy with greed.
> There is no one on earth
> who would buy that fool Thneed!"

But the very next minute I proved he was wrong.
For, just at that minute, a chap came along,
and he thought that the Thneed I had knitted was great.
He happily bought it for three ninety-eight.

I laughed at the Lorax, "You poor stupid guy!
You never can tell what some people will buy."

"I repeat," cried the Lorax,
"I speak for the trees!"

"I'm busy," I told him.
"Shut up, if you please."

I rushed 'cross the room, and in no time at all,
built a radio-phone. I put in a quick call.
I called all my brothers and uncles and aunts
and I said, "Listen here! Here's a wonderful chance
for the whole Once-ler Family to get mighty rich!
Get over here fast! Take the road to North Nitch.
Turn left at Weehawken. Sharp right at South Stitch."

And, in no time at all,
in the factory I built,
the whole Once-ler Family
was working full tilt.
We were all knitting Thneeds
just as busy as bees,
to the sound of the chopping
of Truffula Trees.

Then . . .
Oh! Baby! Oh!
How my business did grow!
Now, chopping one tree
at a time
was too slow.

So I quickly invented my Super-Axe-Hacker
which whacked off four Truffula Trees at one smacker.
We were making Thneeds
four times as fast as before!
And that Lorax? . . .
He didn't show up any more.

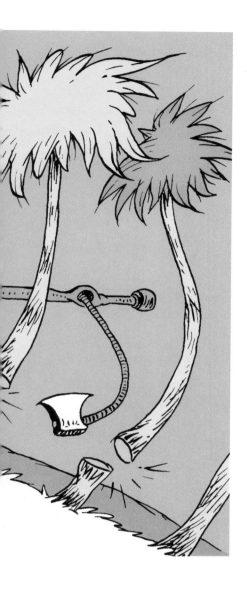

But the next week
he knocked
on my new office door.

He snapped, "I'm the Lorax who speaks for the trees
which you seem to be chopping as fast as you please.
But I'm *also* in charge of the Brown Bar-ba-loots
who played in the shade in their Bar-ba-loot suits
and happily lived, eating Truffula Fruits.

"NOW... thanks to your hacking my trees to the ground,
there's not enough Truffula Fruit to go 'round.
And my poor Bar-ba-loots are all getting the crummies
because they have gas, and no food, in their tummies!

"They loved living here. But I can't let them stay.
They'll have to find food. And I hope that they may.
Good luck, boys," he cried. And he sent them away.

I, the Once-ler, felt sad
as I watched them all go.
BUT...
business is business!
And business must grow
regardless of crummies in tummies, you know.

I meant no harm. I most truly did not.
But I had to grow bigger. So bigger I got.
I biggered my factory. I biggered my roads.
I biggered my wagons. I biggered the loads
of the Thneeds I shipped out. I was shipping them forth
to the South! To the East! To the West! To the North!
I went right on biggering . . . selling more Thneeds.
And I biggered my money, which everyone needs.

Then *again* he came back! I was fixing some pipes
when that old-nuisance Lorax came back with *more* gripes.

"I am the Lorax," he coughed and he whiffed.
He sneezed and he snuffled. He snarggled. He sniffed.
"Once-ler!" he cried with a cruffulous croak.
"Once-ler! You're making such smogulous smoke!
My poor Swomee-Swans . . . why, they can't sing a note!
No one can sing who has smog in his throat.

"And so," said the Lorax,
"—please pardon my cough—
they cannot live here.
So I'm sending them off.

"Where will they go? . . .
I don't hopefully know.

They may have to fly for a month . . . or a year . . .
To escape from the smog you've smogged-up around here.

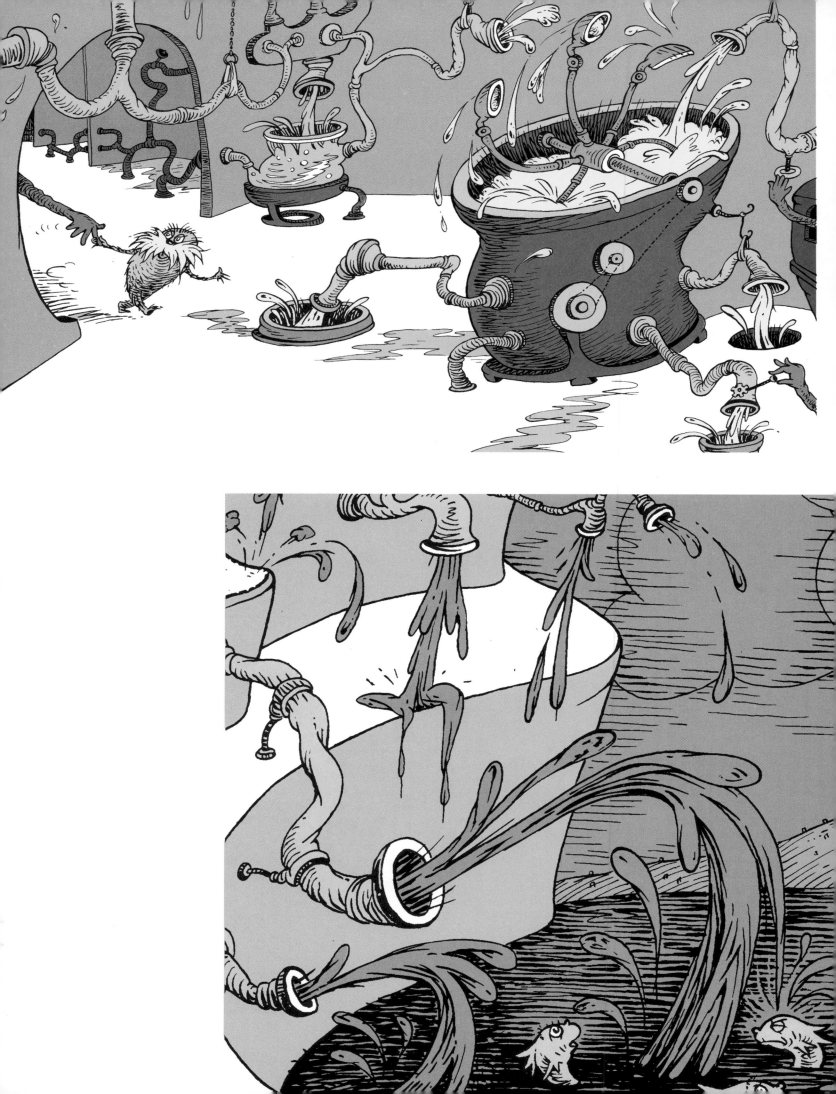

"What's *more*," snapped the Lorax. (His dander was up.)
"Let me say a few words about Gluppity-Glupp.
Your machinery chugs on, day and night without stop
making Gluppity-Glupp. Also Schloppity-Schlopp.
And what do you do with this leftover goo? . . .
I'll show you. You dirty old Once-ler man, you!

"You're glumping the pond where the Humming-Fish hummed!
No more can they hum, for their gills are all gummed.
So I'm sending them off. Oh, their future is dreary.
They'll walk on their fins and get woefully weary
in search of some water that isn't so smeary."

And then I got mad.
I got terribly mad.
I yelled at the Lorax, "Now listen here, Dad!
All you do is yap-yap and say, 'Bad! Bad! Bad! Bad!'
Well, I have my rights, sir, and I'm telling *you*
I intend to go on doing just what I do!
And, for your information, you Lorax, I'm figgering
on biggering

and BIGGERING

and BIGGERING

and BIGGERING,

turning MORE Truffula Trees into Thneeds
which everyone, EVERYONE, *EVERYONE* needs!"

And at that very moment, we heard a loud whack!
From outside in the fields came a sickening smack
of an axe on a tree. Then we heard the tree fall.
The very last Truffula Tree of them all!

No more trees. No more Thneeds. No more work to be done.
So, in no time, my uncles and aunts, every one,
all waved me good-bye. They jumped into my cars
and drove away under the smoke-smuggered stars.

Now all that was left 'neath the bad-smelling sky
was my big empty factory . . .
the Lorax . . .
and I.

The Lorax said nothing. Just gave me a glance . . .
just gave me a very sad, sad backward glance . . .
as he lifted himself by the seat of his pants.
And I'll never forget the grim look on his face
when he heisted himself and took leave of this place,
through a hole in the smog, without leaving a trace.

And all that the Lorax left here in this mess
was a small pile of rocks, with the one word . . .
"UNLESS."
Whatever *that* meant, well, I just couldn't guess.

That was long, long ago.
But each day since that day
I've sat here and worried
and worried away.
Through the years, while my buildings
have fallen apart,
I've worried about it
with all of my heart.

"But *now,*" says the Once-ler,
"Now that *you're* here,
the word of the Lorax seems perfectly clear.
UNLESS someone like you
cares a whole awful lot,
nothing is going to get better.
It's not.

"SO . . .
Catch!" calls the Once-ler.
He lets something fall.
"It's a Truffula Seed.
It's the last one of all!
You're in charge of the last of the Truffula Seeds.
And Truffula Trees are what everyone needs.
Plant a new Truffula. Treat it with care.
Give it clean water. And feed it fresh air.
Grow a forest. Protect it from axes that hack.
Then the Lorax
and all of his friends
may come back."

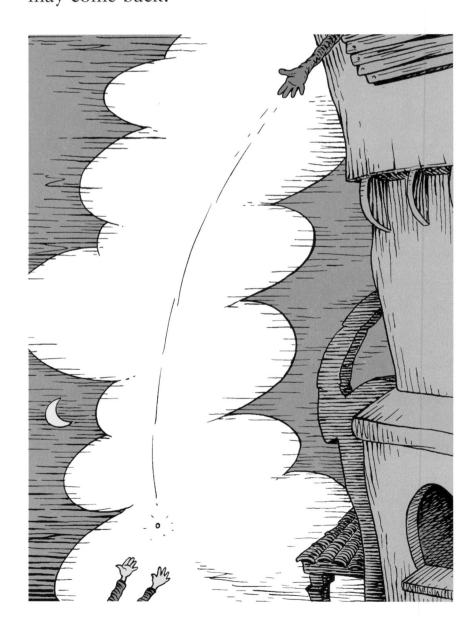

"Cat Detective in the Wrong Part of Town,"
pencil and watercolor on illustration board, 1969.

From *I Had Trouble in Getting to Solla Sollew,* 1965.

SEUSS THE ARCHITECT

*Ted Geisel created buildings
on paper or canvas that
would have been the envy
of Antonio Gaudí. Or, as
Maurice Sendak wrote in
his introduction to* The
Secret Art of Dr. Seuss,
*"The slippery, sloppery,
curvy, altogether
delicious Art Deco
palazzos invite you to
slide and bump along,
in and out of flaming colored mazes. . . .
Ah! The architecture—playing with a sensuous,
loony physicality that re-creates the gleaming,
rapturous infant domain, where various
openings are to be seriously investigated and
explored. All this tricked out with enormous
technical panache: Seuss the Craftsman working
hard to make you forget Seuss the craftsman."*

From *On
Beyond
Zebra!,*
1955.

"O Solo Meow," oil on canvas, 1967.

From *Did I Ever Tell You How Lucky You Are?,* 1973.

living with the cat

Living with Ted was a little like living with the Cat. Ted was tall and lanky. He wore big bow ties, and there was always an air of elegance about him that belied his ongoing potential for mischief, pranks, and the unexpected. While he created laughter for everyone who knew him, his own response was more often than not just his quiet, steady smile.

Ted completed his last book, *Oh, the Places You'll Go!*, about two years before he died. Though his health was failing, he forged ahead with that book in much the same way that he had done with all the others, working late at night once he had his story line. His optimism then was as undaunted as that of the narrator of the book, who declares, "Today is your day! Your mountain is waiting. So . . . *get on your way!*" But I think he realized unconsciously that *Oh, the Places You'll Go!* might be his last book. It turned out to be a summation of his art and ideas and in some ways his own life, which had its ups and downs but through determination did succeed. He completed the book from start to finish in a much shorter period of time than *The Cat in the Hat* and many of his other works, but he was too weak to travel to New York to deliver the ink drawings, as he always had in the past. So Cathy Goldsmith, his Random House art director, came to our house, armed with pages showing hundreds of ink swatches, and Ted picked the precise hue he wanted for every square inch of his drawings.

The book was published on his birthday in 1990 and soon shot to number one on the *New York Times* bestseller list. At that time the *New York Times* did not have a separate bestseller list for children's books, so Ted was especially pleased that it had beat out all of the books that grown-ups buy. Something else that tickled Ted was learning from his editor, Janet Schulman, that *Oh, the Places You'll Go!* was read at her daughter's commencement ceremony in the hallowed halls of the University of Chicago that May. Since then it has become standard fare at hundreds of graduation exercises.

The reception it got energized Ted to write a screenplay based on *Oh, the Places You'll Go!* But his vision for it, which was perhaps more like *Fantasia* than the type of family entertainment now fashionable in Hollywood, never went into production. In spite of this disappointment and his failing health, Ted never lost his sense of humor. One morning a week or so before he died, when I went into his studio, where we had made his sofa into a bed, he opened his eyes and said, "Am I dead yet?" And still with that mischievous smile.

It gives me comfort to know that though his voice was silenced in 1991, his books still speak to millions, keeping his unique sense of humor and humanity alive and well.

AUDREY GEISEL

widow of Theodor S. Geisel

oh, the places you'll go!

[ORIGINALLY PUBLISHED IN 1990]

Congratulations!
Today is your day.
You're off to Great Places!
You're off and away!

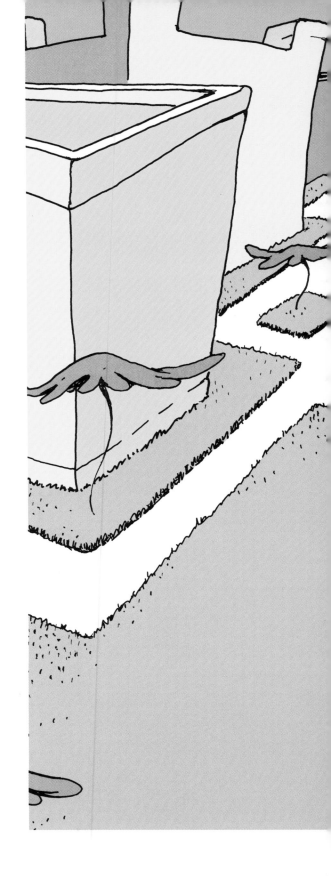

You have brains in your head.
You have feet in your shoes.
You can steer yourself
any direction you choose.
You're on your own. And you know what you know.
And *YOU* are the guy who'll decide where to go.

You'll look up and down streets. Look 'em over with care.
About some you will say, "I don't choose to go there."
With your head full of brains and your shoes full of feet,
you're too smart to go down any not-so-good street.

And you may not find *any*
you'll want to go down.
In that case, of course,
you'll head straight out of town.

It's opener there
in the wide open air.

343

Out there things can happen
and frequently do
to people as brainy
and footsy as you.

And when things start to happen,
don't worry. Don't stew.
Just go right along.
You'll start happening too.

OH!
THE PLACES YOU'LL GO!

You'll be on your way up!
You'll be seeing great sights!
You'll join the high fliers
who soar to high heights.

You won't lag behind, because you'll have the speed.
You'll pass the whole gang and you'll soon take the lead.
Wherever you fly, you'll be best of the best.
Wherever you go, you will top all the rest.

Except when you *don't*.
Because, sometimes, you *won't*.

I'm sorry to say so
but, sadly, it's true
that Bang-ups
and Hang-ups
can happen to you.

You can get all hung up
in a prickle-ly perch.
And your gang will fly on.
You'll be left in a Lurch.

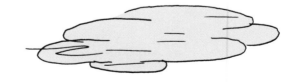

You'll come down from the Lurch
with an unpleasant bump.
And the chances are, then,
that you'll be in a Slump.

And when you're in a Slump,
you're not in for much fun.
Un-slumping yourself
is not easily done.

You will come to a place where the streets are not marked.
Some windows are lighted. But mostly they're darked.
A place you could sprain both your elbow and chin!
Do you dare to stay out? Do you dare to go in?
How much can you lose? How much can you win?

And *IF* you go in, should you turn left or right . . .
or right-and-three-quarters? Or, maybe, not quite?
Or go around back and sneak in from behind?
Simple it's not, I'm afraid you will find,
for a mind-maker-upper to make up his mind.

You can get so confused
that you'll start in to race
down long wiggled roads at a break-necking pace
and grind on for miles across weirdish wild space,
headed, I fear, toward a most useless place.

The Waiting Place . . .

...for people just waiting.
    Waiting for a train to go
    or a bus to come, or a plane to go
    or the mail to come, or the rain to go
    or the phone to ring, or the snow to snow
    or waiting around for a Yes or No
    or waiting for their hair to grow.
    Everyone is just waiting.

    Waiting for the fish to bite
    or waiting for wind to fly a kite
    or waiting around for Friday night
    or waiting, perhaps, for their Uncle Jake
    or a pot to boil, or a Better Break
    or a string of pearls, or a pair of pants
    or a wig with curls, or Another Chance.
    Everyone is just waiting.

NO!
That's not for you!

Somehow you'll escape
all that waiting and staying.
You'll find the bright places
where Boom Bands are playing.

With banner flip-flapping,
once more you'll ride high!
Ready for anything under the sky.
Ready because you're that kind of a guy!

Oh, the places you'll go! There is fun to be done!
There are points to be scored. There are games to be won.
And the magical things you can do with that ball
will make you the winning-est winner of all.
Fame! You'll be famous as famous can be,
with the whole wide world watching you win on TV.

Except when they don't.
Because, sometimes, they won't.

I'm afraid that *some* times
you'll play lonely games too.
Games you can't win
'cause you'll play against you.

All Alone!
Whether you like it or not,
Alone will be something
you'll be quite a lot.

And when you're alone, there's a very good chance
you'll meet things that scare you right out of your pants.
There are some, down the road between hither and yon,
that can scare you so much you won't want to go on.

But on you will go
though the weather be foul.
On you will go
though your enemies prowl.
On you will go
though the Hakken-Kraks howl.
Onward up many
a frightening creek,
though your arms may get sore
and your sneakers may leak.

On and on you will hike.
And I know you'll hike far
and face up to your problems
whatever they are.

You'll get mixed up, of course,
as you already know.
You'll get mixed up
with many strange birds as you go.
So be sure when you step.
Step with care and great tact
and remember that Life's
a Great Balancing Act.
Just never forget to be dexterous and deft.
And *never* mix up your right foot with your left.

And will you succeed?
Yes! You will, indeed!
(98 and 3/4 percent guaranteed.)

KID, YOU'LL MOVE MOUNTAINS!

So...
be your name Buxbaum or Bixby or Bray
or Mordecai Ali Van Allen O'Shea,
you're off to Great Places!
Today is your day!
Your mountain is waiting.
So... *get on your way!*

<u>Commencement Address</u>
<u>Lake Forest College, June 4, 1977</u>

It seems to be behooven upon me to bring forth Great words of wisdom to this graduating class as it leaves these cloistered halls to enter the Outside World beyond.

Fortunately for you of the graduating class, my wisdom is in very short subbly. And I have managed to condense everything I know into an epic poem consisting of 14 lines.

If I can find it under these robes, I will read it quickly and then sit down.

The Epic poem is entitled:

<u>My Uncle Terwilliger on the Art of Eating Popovers</u>

My uncle ordered popovers
from the restaurant's bill of fare.
And, when they were served,
he regarded them
with a penetrating stare...
Then he spoke great words of wisdom
as he sat there on that chair:

"To eat these things,"
said my uncle,
"you must exercise great care.
You may swallow down what's solid....
BUT...
you must spit out the air!" —

***

And...
as you partake of the world's bill of fare,
that's darned good advice to follow.
Do a lot of spitting out the hot air.
And be careful what you swallow.

books written and illustrated by dr. seuss

And to Think That I Saw It on Mulberry Street, 1937

The 500 Hats of Bartholomew Cubbins, 1938

The King's Stilts, 1939

Horton Hatches the Egg, 1940

McElligot's Pool, 1947

Thidwick the Big-Hearted Moose, 1948

Bartholomew and the Oobleck, 1949

If I Ran the Zoo, 1950

Scrambled Eggs Super!, 1953

Horton Hears a Who!, 1954

On Beyond Zebra!, 1955

If I Ran the Circus, 1956

How the Grinch Stole Christmas!, 1957

The Cat in the Hat, 1957

The Cat in the Hat Comes Back, 1958

Yertle the Turtle and Other Stories, 1958

Happy Birthday to You!, 1959

Green Eggs and Ham, 1960

One Fish Two Fish Red Fish Blue Fish, 1960

The Sneetches and Other Stories, 1961

Dr. Seuss's Sleep Book, 1962

Hop on Pop, 1962

If I Ran the Circus

The 500 Hats of Bartholomew Cubbins

On Beyond Zebra!

Scrambled Eggs Super!

*I Can Lick
30 Tigers Today!*

*I Had Trouble in Getting
to Solla Sollew*

Dr. Seuss's ABC, 1963

Fox in Socks, 1965

I Had Trouble in Getting to Solla Sollew, 1965

The Cat in the Hat Songbook, 1967

The Foot Book, 1968

I Can Lick 30 Tigers Today! and Other Stories, 1969

I Can Draw It Myself, 1970

Mr. Brown Can Moo! Can You?, 1970

The Lorax, 1971

Marvin K. Mooney Will You Please Go Now!, 1972

The Shape of Me and Other Stuff, 1973

Did I Ever Tell You How Lucky You Are?, 1973

There's a Wocket in My Pocket!, 1974

Oh, the Thinks You Can Think!, 1975

The Cat's Quizzer, 1976

I Can Read with My Eyes Shut!, 1978

Oh Say Can You Say?, 1979

Hunches in Bunches, 1982

The Butter Battle Book, 1984

You're Only Old Once!, 1986

Oh, the Places You'll Go!, 1990

The Butter Battle Book

Image details are listed by page number (in **bold**), from left to right, top to bottom.

2. Dr. Seuss, *The Sneetches and Other Stories* (New York: Random House, 1961). **3.** Dr. Seuss, *The Cat in the Hat* (New York: Random House, 1957); Dr. Seuss, *And to Think That I Saw It on Mulberry Street* (New York: Random House, 1937). **4.** Dr. Seuss, *Oh, the Places You'll Go!* (New York: Random House, 1990). **5.** Dr. Seuss, *Horton Hears a Who!* (New York: Random House, 1954). **6.** Photo of Ted at drawing board (1978), copyright © by E. T. Masterson; Ted's senior-yearbook portrait, *Pnalka*. **7.** Ted and a feline friend, *Telechronicle* 3, no. 11 (February 1932): inside front cover; Ted at a reception, from the private collection of Mrs. Audrey S. Geisel. **8.** Ted as a toddler, from the private collection of Mrs. Audrey S. Geisel; Ted with Theophrastus (circa 1910), copyright © 2002 by Margaretha D. Owens and Theodor B. Owens; Ted at the beach with father and sister, Marnie (circa 1907), copyright © 2002 by Margaretha D. Owens and Theodor B. Owens; Ted after fishing (circa 1919), copyright © 2002 by Margaretha D. Owens and Theodor B. Owens; Ted with Dartmouth classmates, courtesy of the Dr. Seuss Collection, Mandeville Special Collections Library, University of California, San Diego. **9.** Ted in military uniform (circa January 1943), copyright © 2002 by Margaretha D. Owens and Theodor B. Owens; Ted posed against landscape, from the private collection of Mrs. Audrey S. Geisel; Ted at desk with first wife, Helen (June 21, 1953), copyright © San Diego Historical Society; still photo D-8064-P38 of Tommy Rettig in Ted Geisel's lap during the making of *The 5000 Fingers of Dr. T,* courtesy of Sony Pictures Entertainment; Ted with some of his "secret art," courtesy of the Dr. Seuss Collection, Mandeville Special Collections Library, University of California, San Diego; Ted on parade, courtesy of the Dr. Seuss Collection, Mandeville Special Collections Library, University of California, San Diego; Ted (1978), from the private collection of Mrs. Audrey S. Geisel. **10.** Dr. Seuss, *And to Think That I Saw It on Mulberry Street* (New York: Random House, 1937). **23.** Photo of 74 Fairfield Street taken in 2002, from the private collection of Charles D. Cohen; Ted, age four, in 74 Fairfield Street yard (1908), copyright © 2002 by Margaretha D. Owens and Theodor B. Owens; the Cat in the Hat sculpture, courtesy of The Springfield Museums, copyright © 2002–2004 by Dr. Seuss Enterprises, L.P.; postcard of the Springfield, Massachusetts, Main Street arch, from the private collection of Charles D. Cohen. **24.** Dr. Seuss, *McElligot's Pool* (New York: Random House, 1947). **55.** Dr. Seuss, *One Fish Two Fish Red Fish Blue Fish* (New York: Random House, 1960); *Secrets of the Deep, Vol. II* (July 1936): front cover; Dr. Seuss, *One Fish Two Fish Red Fish Blue Fish* (New York: Random House, 1960); *Secrets of the Deep, Vol. II* (July 1936): 32; *Secrets of the Deep* (June 1934): 15; Dr. Seuss, *One Fish Two Fish Red Fish Blue Fish* (New York: Random House, 1960); *Secrets of the Deep, Vol. II* (July 1936): 25; Dr. Seuss, *Hop on Pop* (New York: Random House, 1963). **56.** Dr. Seuss, *If I Ran the Zoo* (New York: Random House, 1950). **83.** Images copyright © by Dr. Seuss Enterprises, L.P. **84.** Dr. Seuss, *Horton Hears a Who!* (New York: Random House, 1954). **117.** NBC Radio advertisements, courtesy of General Electric; *Judge* 94, no. 2411 (January 14, 1928): 16; Flit subway card, woman in hat with mosquitoes (1947); Essolube advertisement, "Foil the Karbo-nockus!" (January 1933); Holly Sugar advertising campaign (1954–56); Vico motor oil billboard (circa August 1938). **118.** Dr. Seuss, *The Cat in the Hat* (New York: Random House, 1957). **157.** Copyright © by Dr. Seuss Enterprises, L.P.; three preliminary drawings for *The Cat in the Hat Songbook,* courtesy of the collection of the Department of Special Collections, University Research Library, University of California, Los Angeles. **158.** Dr. Seuss, *How the Grinch Stole Christmas!* (New York: Random House, 1957). **189.** *Redbook* story, copyright © by Dr. Seuss Enterprises, L.P.; *Redbook* 110, no. 2 (October 1957): table of contents; Grinch license plate, courtesy of Kristin Lundgren Macari; Ted and Chuck Jones, courtesy of the Dr. Seuss Collection, Mandeville Special Collections Library, University of California, San Diego. **190.** Dr. Seuss, *Yertle the Turtle and Other Stories* (New York: Random House, 1950). **207.** World War II cartoons, from the private collection of Charles D. Cohen. **208.** Dr. Seuss, *Happy Birthday to You!* (New York: Random House, 1959). **235.** *Life* 101, no. 2590 (May 1934): cover; *Judge* 104, no. 2655 (June 1933): cover; 1935 calendar art series: "Seein' Things" (Jan.–Aug.); Dr. Seuss, *Yertle the Turtle and Other Stories* (New York: Random House, 1950); Dr. Seuss, *Horton Hatches the Egg* (New York: Random House, 1940); painting copyright © by Dr. Seuss Enterprises, L.P.; Dr. Seuss, *Scrambled Eggs Super!* (New York: Random House, 1953). **236.** Dr. Seuss, *Green Eggs and Ham* (New York: Random House, 1960). **263.** From draft of *Green Eggs and Ham,* by Dr. Seuss. Image courtesy of the Dr. Seuss Collection, Mandeville Special Collections Library, University of California, San Diego. *Green Eggs and Ham* copyright © 1960, renewed 1988 by Dr. Seuss Enterprises, L.P. **264.** Dr. Seuss, *The Sneetches and Other Stories* (New York: Random House, 1961). **281.** Dr. Seuss, *Oh, the Thinks You Can Think!* (New York: Random House, 1975); Dr. Seuss, *The Butter Battle Book* (New York: Random House, 1984); Dr. Seuss, *Did I Ever Tell You How Lucky You Are?* (New York: Random House, 1973); Dr. Seuss, *You're Only Old Once!* (New York: Random House, 1986); Daggett & Ramsdell advertisement, Lambs of St. Patrick's Dinner, Gambol, and Ball program (March 17, 1934): 16. **282.** Dr. Seuss, *Dr. Seuss's Sleep Book* (New York: Random House, 1962). **303.** First page of manuscript from three different drafts of *Dr. Seuss's Sleep Book,* by Dr. Seuss. Images courtesy of the Dr. Seuss Collection, Mandeville Special Collections Library, University of California, San Diego. *Dr. Seuss's Sleep Book,* copyright © 1962, renewed 1990 by Dr. Seuss Enterprises, L.P. **304.** Dr. Seuss, *The Lorax* (New York: Random House, 1971). **337.** Painting copyright © by Dr. Seuss Enterprises, L.P.; Dr. Seuss, *I Had Trouble in Getting to Solla Sollew* (New York: Random House, 1965); Dr. Seuss, *On Beyond Zebra!* (New York: Random House, 1955); painting copyright © by Dr. Seuss Enterprises, L.P.; Dr. Seuss, *Did I Ever Tell You How Lucky You Are?* (New York: Random House, 1973). **338.** Dr. Seuss, *Oh, the Places You'll Go!* (New York: Random House, 1990). **365.** Commencement address draft, from the private collection of Mrs. Audrey S. Geisel. **366.** Dr. Seuss, *If I Ran the Circus* (New York: Random House, 1956); Dr. Seuss, *The 500 Hats of Bartholomew Cubbins* (New York: Random House, 1938); Dr. Seuss, *Scrambled Eggs Super!* (New York: Random House, 1953); Dr. Seuss, *On Beyond Zebra!* (New York: Random House, 1955). **367.** Dr. Seuss, *I Can Lick 30 Tigers Today! And Other Stories* (New York: Random House, 1969); Dr. Seuss, *I Had Trouble in Getting to Solla Sollew* (New York: Random House, 1965); Dr. Seuss, *The Butter Battle Book* (New York: Random House, 1984); Dr. Seuss, *The Cat in the Hat Comes Back* (New York: Random House, 1958). **368.** Dr. Seuss, *Dr. Seuss's Sleep Book* (New York: Random House, 1962).